Islands Apart

Islands
Apart

Eva McColl

Copyright © 2023 Eva McColl

The moral right of the author has been asserted.

Apart from any fair dealing for the purposes of research or private study, or criticism or review, as permitted under the Copyright, Designs and Patents Act 1988, this publication may only be reproduced, stored or transmitted, in any form or by any means, with the prior permission in writing of the publishers, or in the case of reprographic reproduction in accordance with the terms of licences issued by the Copyright Licensing Agency. Enquiries concerning reproduction outside those terms should be sent to the publishers.

This is a work of fiction. Names, characters, businesses, places, events and incidents are either the products of the author's imagination or used in a fictitious manner. Any resemblance to actual persons, living or dead, or actual events is purely coincidental.

Matador
Unit E2 Airfield Business Park
Harrison Road, Market Harborough
Leicestershire LE16 7UL
Tel: 0116 279 2299
Email: books@troubador.co.uk
Web: www.troubador.co.uk/matador
Twitter: @matadorbooks

ISBN 978-1-80514-084-9

British Library Cataloguing in Publication Data.
A catalogue record for this book is available from the British Library.

Printed and bound by CPI Group (UK) Ltd, Croydon, CR0 4YY
Typeset in 11pt Minion Pro by Troubador Publishing Ltd, Leicester, UK

Matador is an imprint of Troubador Publishing Ltd

For Brian, Karl, Karin, Jess and Laura.

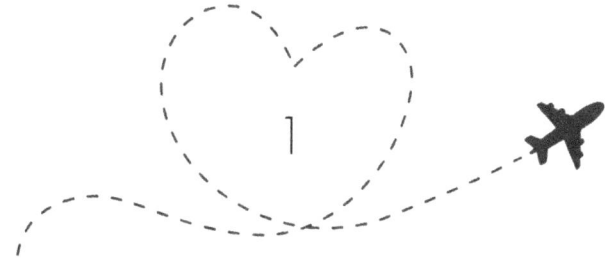

1

It was just after 2 p.m. when the British Airways flight from London touched down in Barbados. Laura Stevens felt the midday heat engulf her face as she walked slowly across the tarmac. The vein of caution that life had taught her continued to trouble her as she entered the terminal building. She said goodbye to her fellow travellers as they collected their luggage, wishing them a good holiday. Scanning the waiting crowd, she looked anxiously for a sign with her name on it but saw none.

Suddenly she felt a touch on her shoulder and her heart leapt. Turning around, she saw that in front of her was a tall, handsome young man, his lightly tanned skin in marked contrast to her own milky-white complexion. His surfy-style dark hair reached the collar of his white shirt.

"You must be Laura Stevens," he ventured, checking the photograph in his hand.

"Yes, I am," she replied, puzzled.

"I'm Blake Degas, a friend of the MacIvers. They

were unable to come to the airport to meet you… so I volunteered," he explained. "Welcome to Barbados!"

Picking up the suitcases, he led her towards the large glass doors of the exit.

"How was your flight?" he enquired as she followed him to his car. His soft American accent charmed her.

"Fine, thank you," she answered. "Whereabouts in the States are you from?" she asked, getting into his navy-blue Mercedes.

"New York but I live here in Barbados. I have a beach house on the west coast. I like it down here. My job allows me to live where I want."

"Lucky you. How come?" asked Laura.

"I'm a pilot with a freight company," he smiled. "We fly the Caribbean and America."

As they left the airport, Laura looked at him reflectively. She guessed he would be about thirty years old, a few years older than her.

"You look too young to be flying around the world as a pilot," she teased.

"I got a helluva lot of flying hours in the US Air Force," he explained.

Laura took a long hard look at Blake as she sat beside him in the car. His brooding good looks intrigued her. Long, dark lashes and eyebrows framed his deep brown eyes. His strong jawline was softened only by sensual lips. She noticed his tanned, muscular arms and long fingers gripping the steering wheel. This was not the welcome she had expected, but it was nevertheless a very pleasant one.

"Is yours a Scottish accent?" Blake asked.

Laura nodded. "Close enough," she laughed.

"It sings a little," he said, turning towards her and smiling. "I like that."

Laura looked out of the car window with interest. They drove past rows of little wooden houses that reminded her of the gingerbread house in the fairy tale.

"They're called Chattel houses," Blake commented, as if reading her thoughts. "When a family wants more space, they simply add on an extra room to the back of the house. Over there you can see the fields of sugar cane."

On the left, the road followed the contour of the Caribbean Sea. Beaches of white, glistening sand stretched like a ribbon beside the calm turquoise waters. Laura's thoughts flashed back to the island she had left behind. Rows of neat, grey, stone cottages and houses nestled beside the ruins of an ancient priory, once the cradle of Christianity in the sixth century. She pictured the castle high on a crag, reaching like a dark shadow into the sky over the cold waters of the North Sea, reminding her of enchanted castles where beautiful princesses sleep for a hundred years.

Holy Island had been home since she was three years old. That was when her parents had been killed in a car accident in Edinburgh and she had gone to live on the island with her widowed grandmother. She knew very little about her parents. Whenever she asked questions, her grandmother would be evasive, putting up a defensive barrier. As a child, an overwhelming worry that her grandmother would leave too pervaded Laura's mind and she learnt not to ask. However, Holy Island had given her roots and she had been content until recently, when a series of events had turned her world upside down.

Firstly, David had asked her to marry him. He was also a child of the island. They had grown up together and had been close friends since high school. David was ambitious and never faltered from his wish to become a doctor. He was an only child and his parents were understandably very proud of him. Handsome, with tousled fair hair and serious grey eyes, Laura always felt he had the appearance of a well-loved country doctor. Her grandmother thought David had the attributes of a good husband and often told Laura so. There was no fanciful romance here, it was friendship, but nevertheless that was considered to be a good base for marriage by the islanders. Life on Holy Island was like that... predictable! She loved David, but it wasn't the love she dreamed of. Laura had declined his offer. They were best friends but marriage – that was something else.

Then, her grandmother became ill and Laura left her teaching post in Edinburgh to return to Holy Island to look after her. Shortly before her grandmother died, she called Laura into her bedroom and fixed her with her pale, rheumy eyes. Her demeanour was different. On the bed was a box containing papers and photographs.

"Your mother was beautiful, Laura, but she had a wild streak. Rose dreamt of travelling to glamorous places she'd only read about. Our island was never enough for her." She looked into Laura's face expectantly.

"I always loved this picture of you in Barbados... you all look so happy. It has given me so much comfort over the years," she gave a deep sigh, her voice hardly louder than a whisper.

Laura took the photograph. It was of a small child, presumably herself, with her parents Rose and John, sitting under a tree with the sea in the distance. Laura quietly seated herself on the bed and gazed intently at the photograph, the only one she had seen of herself with her parents. She was filled with a deep sense of loss. Written on the back was *Underneath the breadfruit tree at Paradise*.

Her grandmother spoke softly. "They loved living there and in three years only made one fateful trip back here to see me."

"I didn't know we lived there." Laura's voice was hollow.

"I should have told you. I feel ashamed, I locked the past away." Tears began to roll down her grandmother's cheeks.

They were the first gentle words Laura had ever heard about her parents and tears welled up in her eyes. She began sifting through the contents of the box, idly picking up first one letter, then another, moving them around as if her hands needed to be occupied. Then, gathering up the box in her arms, she straightened up.

"I'm sorry," her grandmother whispered.

Laura remained silent. Kissing her grandmother softly on the forehead, she left the room. She shuddered at the complex emotions that had been aroused in her: resentment mingled with compassion for her grandmother.

A week had elapsed after her grandmother's death before Laura had tentatively opened the drawer of her bedside cabinet and taken out the box of letters. She placed it on the bed and removed the lid, picking up a silver photo frame and opening it. On one side was a wedding photo of her parents, smiling proudly and looking very happy: on the other side, a picture of herself sitting on her mother's lap, wearing a floral dress and a sun hat to match. It must have been taken on her birthday, because a big badge on her dress read *I am 2*. Laura put the frame on top of her cabinet and took a lingering look at the photos. It was the first time she had ever seen them. Her hands trembled as she picked up notelets with pictures of Barbados on the front and short messages inside.

"Dear Mam, we are really enjoying ourselves here. We have made friends and meet them for lunch on Sundays at the Abbeyville. I love the banana daiquiris there and Laura swims in the pool. We hope you can come and stay with us. We will gladly send you the airfare. Please consider coming."

"Dear Mam, so sorry you don't want to come to Barbados. We understand. Have sent you a photo of Laura on her first trip to the beach. She loved it and ran around with joy. She is so independent and sociable. We miss you."

The most poignant of all for Laura read, *"Dear Mam, we are coming home for three weeks. John is renewing his contract for three years. We will be together soon. You and Laura will be able to spend time together. I can't wait."*

Laura had read enough. Her heart was heavy with sadness and disappointment. There were so many memories that her grandmother could have shared that told a little girl how much she was loved. *Then again*, she thought, *who am I to judge?* Who knows how any of us would react to such a tragedy?

Several days after the funeral, David had come down again from Edinburgh to see her. Arriving at the cottage, he gave her a much-needed hug.

"You look pale," he said. "Let's get out of here – you need to walk."

Laura hoped the stifling atmosphere of the cottage would dissipate into the cool of the afternoon air, but as she walked through the narrow streets they seemed to be crowding her in. They strolled to the beach. The tide was high and the turbulent waters of the North Sea looked dark and mysterious, the rhythmic crashes of the white horses endless. Above them the piercing cries of the seagulls echoed along the deserted shoreline, their white wings contrasting against the grey of the sky.

As they had walked, David talked about what he'd been doing. While she listened, Laura felt she wanted to tell him how she was feeling since her grandmother died. How lonely she felt, how restless she had become, how curiosity about her past had reared its head. She very much wanted to talk to him, but David seemed pre-occupied with work, so she thought better of it.

Leaving the sands, they took a route through the gentle hills past the upturned herring boats towards the cliffs of the cove. The turf was thinner here, appearing to Laura like a green sheet thrown over the rocks. Reaching the top, they sat down. Shivering, Laura pulled up the collar of her coat and gazed out towards the horizon.

"Remember when we used to come up here as kids? It felt so wild," she said wistfully.

"It hasn't changed much," said David. "That's what I

love about our island." David could hold back no longer. "There's something I want to tell you Laura."

Her heart beat fast at the urgent tone of his voice.

"I've been offered a permanent post at the hospital," he said, with a mixture of modesty and satisfaction. "They're pleased with the progress I've made and think I'll fit in well with the team."

"That's wonderful, David. Congratulations."

"I'm in a good position now to settle down. I can move out of the house share and get a flat in Edinburgh. When you come back you could move in with me. I'll be able to cover the rent." His voice was touchingly eager.

She looked straight ahead; she was stunned. She didn't want her life mapped out for her like that. She had felt "settled down" all her life. When her friends went off travelling to Thailand or the almost obligatory gap year in Australia, Laura spent her holidays on Holy Island. Her grandmother was getting frail. It was what Laura wanted, and she felt it was the right thing to do. But now...

"I'm not sure I'm going back to Edinburgh, David," she said quietly. "I have other plans."

"What other plans?" he asked.

Laura moved a little away from him, pushing her hair back from her forehead with a trembling hand. She gave David a steady look. "I want to go to Barbados."

"What on earth for?" He looked incredulous.

"I would like to see where I lived with my parents."

"Go on holiday," he suggested.

"I want more than that. I feel the need to touch base with my past." Laura needed him to listen; why couldn't he see that she had the right to make choices? Moisture filled her eyes. Feelings of loss washed over her like a fine mist of rain and David didn't seem to understand.

"Come on," he said suddenly. "Let's get going. I have to drive back tonight, I'm afraid."

Laura always knew work came first with David. She wondered if she was expecting too much of him. He had his own pressures at the hospital.

At the cottage, Laura had made tea.

"So let me get this straight," he said. "You're going away?"

"I think so," she said softly.

"Well, I hope you know what you're doing, Laura." He sounded concerned.

Laura felt she'd always been cautious, made sensible decisions. It was as though she was just waking up to her life, perhaps for the first time listening to the inner voice she had been ignoring for years.

"I do," Laura replied, but she really wasn't sure.

"There's always Edinburgh if you change your mind." His voice had faltered. She knew he was hurt. He hugged her tightly and kissed her on the cheek. Then he was gone. Looking up, she had glanced out of the window. It had started to pour with rain. In that moment, she knew she wanted something different, to move away from the mundane, to take a chance in life – after all what was there to lose? Her mind was made up. She would go to Barbados. When she saw an advert in *The Times Ed.* for a temporary teaching post, she applied without a second thought.

As they turned off Bay Street, Blake's voice interrupted

her thoughts. "We're here. I guess you must be tired after your long journey."

A short driveway opened onto a square courtyard. Blake brought the car to a stop in front of a white, double-storey building.

"Orient View, Bay Street; your new address. Liam has arranged for you to have the upstairs apartment."

Getting out of the car, Laura glanced up at the large wooden shutters on the windows. Flamboyant, red and orange trees in full bloom gave shade to the courtyard, the flowers falling in cascades against the white walls.

"This way."

Blake carried her luggage towards the back of the building. Laura followed through an arch and up some wooden stairs to a large veranda. The balmy air was fragrant with the scent of jasmine and frangipani trees. She looked out over a small garden towards the Caribbean Sea, its surface shimmering under the intense sunlight. The freshness of the air intermingled with the musky aroma of this tropical island enveloped her and she felt a thrill of anticipation. Double doors opened onto a large, airy room with louvered windows on each side. Simply furnished, a large, circular rush mat lay in the centre of a polished wood floor. A small table and four chairs fitted snugly in one corner. Brightly coloured cushions were scattered on a large sofa under a window.

"If there's nothing else I can do, I'll leave you to get some rest."

Before she could thank him, Blake was off down the steps to his car. Laura felt strangely bereft. He was a friendly face in her new life and she wanted to call him back but restrained herself. Through the doorway, she caught a glimpse of the deserted bay and could hear the gentle lapping of the waves against the shoreline. Going into the bedroom, she was suddenly overwhelmed by tiredness. She lay down on top of the crisp, white sheets. The splashing of the sea soon lulled her into a deep slumber.

The sun was streaming through the bedroom window when she awoke much later than usual the next morning. For a moment, she lay with her eyes closed, feeling unsure. Slowly, she opened them, and gazed at the unfamiliar objects in the room. Just like remembering a dream, the events of the past weeks came flooding back to her and a wave of fear welled up from deep within her soul. The sensation shocked her. Going through to the small bathroom, she showered, brushed her teeth and dressed, putting on a pink cotton dress over her slender body. As she glanced in the mirror, she saw the reflection of her long, black hair and pale skin. She applied some mascara to the lashes of her dark blue eyes, now looking even bigger and darker in the morning light. She brushed her hair and was spraying a little perfume when a knock on the veranda door startled her. Opening it, she was surprised to see Blake standing there.

"Care to come for a boat ride around the bay, see your new surroundings?" he asked.

Laura hesitated. She felt embarrassed. Once again he had managed to take her by surprise.

"Have you made other arrangements?"

"No, no, of course not." She faltered. "I'll have to come like this." She pointed to her dress. "I haven't unpacked yet."

"Sure, that's fine. You'll need shades and plenty of sunscreen, it will get real hot soon."

As they walked along the beach, Blake asked how she was feeling.

"Fine," came the reply. "Looking forward to a completely different life for a while."

"Well, you've come to the right place. Sunshine all year," he smiled.

"Can't wait," said Laura.

They had now reached a jetty with several small boats moored alongside it. Blake helped her into a shiny blue and white speedboat. Sitting down in the front, Laura surveyed the scene around her with interest. Blake started the engine and the pale Caribbean waters danced around them as they left the bay and headed for the open sea. Before long, they were racing over the calm waters, leaving a foaming white surge of waves in their wake. Laura's mood began to lift. The fresh sea air made her face tingle and her long hair was blowing in the strong breeze. She felt an unprecedented sense of freedom and well-being. Despite growing up beside the sea, she had never before been in a speedboat. On entering a lagoon, Blake stopped the engine and they drifted along silently on the current. Laura leaned over the side and trailed her hand in the water like a child. The surface of the water looked silver in the morning light and beneath the watery mosaic, she could see the glorious colours of tropical fish darting in and out of the coral reef. At this moment in time, she felt there was nowhere in the world she would rather be. Occasionally, a flying fish would leap out and glide along the top of the water to her delight and she would gasp in surprise.

"It's so beautiful here," she said.

"Good for chilling out," he replied.

Looking up, she noticed that Blake had been watching her and she felt a little unnerved. Starting up the motor, he turned the boat back towards the bay and as they approached, Laura could see fishermen mending their nets on the beach, their brightly coloured T-shirts dotted against the white sand. Beyond them in the distance, she recognised Orient View, its white walls gleaming, yet looking different when viewed from the sea. It occurred to Laura that this was going to be true of life from now on… a new perspective. As they re-entered the bay, she glanced at Blake's watch and realised they had been out for well over one and a half hours. She had lost all track of time.

The boat glided towards the shore. They reached the jetty and Blake jumped out and moored the boat. Observing him, Laura sensed there was a restlessness in him beneath his calm exterior. He helped her onto the wet sand, which felt delightfully cool beneath her feet. Enjoying the sensation, she began to walk along the shoreline. The waves pulled around her ankles as they swept back into the sea and her feet sank into the sand. The urge to be in the water was too much. Throwing caution to the wind in a sudden fit of merriment, Laura plunged herself into the warm Caribbean. She surfaced above the swell. Shaking her hair, her blue eyes sparkled and her cheeks were flushed. Blake watched non-plussed; his eyes crinkled into an expression of amusement. Regaining her composure, Laura waded ashore dripping and laughing. She brushed her hands through her wet hair, and they carried on walking to the garden at Orient View. Blake chuckled.

"Feeling better?" he asked.

"I am, as it happens. I couldn't resist it, the warm water felt so inviting. Mind you, I should have hung on to my sunnies," she said, blinking in the sunlight.

Blake found Laura's naturalness refreshing. He had become so used to women with "wet hair phobia".

Before there was time for reflection, a young woman in a bright yellow sundress presented herself, her earnest face set in a frame of unruly brown, curly hair. As she smiled and tilted her head to one side, her brown eyes examined the scene with some amusement.

"Hi, I'm Emma. I live here."

She pointed to the doorway of the downstairs apartment. Laura felt embarrassed as the water from her body dripped onto the patio stone.

"I'm Laura, and this is Blake," she said.

"Good to meet you, Emma." Blake offered a hand, which Emma shook graciously.

"Pleased to meet you both," she said.

"Well, I'm going to leave you two," Blake said politely, making his departure.

Once again, Laura could not explain the sudden emotion she felt as he left.

"He's fit," said Emma, smiling.

"I think he knows it," Laura quipped.

Blake Degas was probably used to women succumbing to his considerable charms and good looks, thought Laura. Reflecting on the morning's events, she had to acknowledge that, despite having arrived less than twenty-four hours ago, this beautiful island was already having an unsettling effect on her.

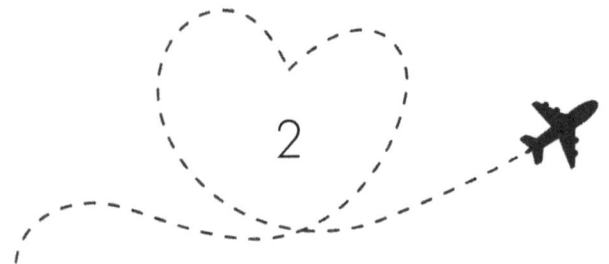

2

Emma came like a breath of fresh air into Laura's life. Having lived in Kent all of her life, she had gone to Barbados on holiday and fallen in love with the island. She decided to move away from the cold winters of the UK and applied for a teaching post at St. Catherine's. One year later, she had renewed her contract and couldn't be happier.

Laura busied herself in the kitchen making coffee for the two of them while Emma opened up about her personal life to date. She was in a relationship with Ivan, a doctor at the local hospital.

"Ivan's mother Carmel has the Yellow Bird Boutique in Oistins. She sells adorable beachwear and kaftans. Her prices are so reasonable, I'll take you there."

"I'd love that," laughed Laura. "I don't have many clothes for the heat."

"So, Laura, what brought you to St. Catherine's?" Emma asked.

Laura smiled.

"Well," she began slowly, "I'd been looking after my grandma. When she died, I felt the need to escape to somewhere completely different. So here I am," she concluded.

"Well, I'm glad you're here," Emma grinned. "Most weeks include a trip to Bridgetown, how about we go on Saturday? Everyone does."

How true that turned out to be!

Saturday arrived and the beginning of another hot day in Barbados. Laura was excited. Emma was taking her on her first visit to Bridgetown. They met early morning in the courtyard as arranged and set off in the direction of Bridgetown, running the gauntlet between a myriad of buses, cars and bicycles on Bay Street; hoots and toots came from all directions.

Each bus appeared full to bursting inside. Through the windows a colourful collage of straw hats and happy faces bobbed to and fro as the bus crawled along, stopped, then crawled again. Young men stood on the outside steps swaying and laughing nonchalantly, hanging on to the rail with one hand. In the midst of it all, cyclists skilfully weaved their way through. There was a feeling of bustle and purpose everywhere and Laura soaked up the vibrancy of it all. It could not be more different to her life on Holy Island.

As there were no sidewalks, they were forced to walk intrepidly alongside the road. The morning warmth soon turned to baking heat. Laura would rather have hopped onto a bus, slow as they were here, but Emma was having none of it, so she pressed on valiantly. As she looked around, it seemed to her that a straw hat, a resigned expression and a slow gait were the order of the day. In a desire to absorb the local colour, Laura popped into the next small supermarket and bought herself a bright red straw hat. She grabbed the nearest one, which turned out to be too big for her and flopped over her face. Emma giggled, but in the now blazing heat, Laura was glad to have it. They took about twenty minutes to arrive at the bridge. Looking down into the Careenage as they crossed, Laura could see two charter fishing boats and several yachts moored there. Finally, they arrived in Bridgetown.

"Every Saturday in Bridgetown the locals go 'liming' – walking around having fun or relaxing with friends, the sole aim being to see and be seen. It's good fun." Emma was eager to familiarise her friend with the ways of the island.

"Is this how you spend Saturdays?" asked Laura incredulously.

"Hell no!" said Emma. "I like to watch from the balcony of the Bridge Bar."

So saying, she took Laura's arm and, crossing the road, led her into a small building and up a narrow staircase to an open New Orleans-style balcony set with tables and chairs. They were greeted warmly by an old Bajan waiter, who pointed them towards two chairs beside one of the tables.

"Fresh up here, isn't it?" remarked Emma.

Fresh? thought Laura; she had never felt such heat

in her whole life. They were the only two on the balcony and to Laura's relief they sat there comfortably with a long drink for quite a while. They watched the throng of people below with interest, their bright clothing giving splashes of colour between the slow-moving traffic. Laura was surprised at how much she was enjoying herself until, suddenly, she thought she caught sight of Blake, the rays of the morning sun reflecting off his white shirt like a spotlight. Holding up the brim of her large straw hat to get a better look, she saw that it was indeed Blake and he was with a tall, blonde woman. He was holding her by the arm. Laura watched as they waited for several cars to pass before they made their way across the street and disappeared into a nearby department store. Laura was astonished at the strange reaction this brought. Her heart began beating in her throat. She tried to tell herself it was not her business what Blake did, she'd only known him for a week, but at the same time she was disappointed. Perhaps Blake Degas was a player and Laura was glad she had found out early in their friendship.

"We should head off now," she heard Emma's voice.

"Yes," said Laura, distracted.

"Before we return," Emma was saying as she stood up to leave, "I want to show you the fruit market."

The market proved to be a real eye-opener for Laura, with row upon row of every fruit she recognised and some she didn't. There was too much choice. Before long, they were carrying large bags of fruit out onto the street. Laura found that shopping had lifted her mood. They set off towards a bus stop. At that very moment, a Mini Moke with two men inside pulled up in front of them. Emma waved and quickened her step to walk over to the open car.

"Wanna lift, ladies?" The driver looked at them, smiling. At the same time, a tall, lean, older man jumped out of the passenger side and took their shopping from them, putting it in the back.

"It hot… hot… hot," he was saying as he helped them into the Moke.

Although confused, Laura glanced at Emma and smiled. She was pleased they didn't have to walk back.

Emma introduced the two men as Marc and Fidel.

"Marc owns the fish market beside us, his daughter Dulcie is in my class. Fidel is her grandpa."

Laura took a good look at the two men who had rescued them. Marc was driving and she was not surprised to hear that he was from Martinique. Dressed in jeans and a navy T-shirt, he wore a black beret sideways over his Afro hairstyle. Even in such simple clothing, he had a certain French chic about him.

Fidel, she guessed, was possibly about sixty years old, and was also sporting jeans and a T-shirt. On his head, he wore a black trilby.

Fidel turned to them. "Yuh bin limin'?" he asked, laughing.

"Of course," replied Emma, "and shopping."

To Laura's relief, the traffic leaving Bridgetown was much lighter and they were soon entering Bay Street when suddenly, Marc steered the Moke onto the side of the road and without warning brought them to a sudden halt. Grabbing a sack from the floor on the passenger side, he leapt out onto the road.

"Oh yeah," exclaimed Fidel, obviously aware of what was happening.

Being curious, Laura stood up and leaned out of the side, looking vaguely into the distance. She took a sharp intake of breath when she saw the biggest crab imaginable walking sideways in the road. It was making a strange sound, a sort of squeaking noise much like a bicycle wheel that needs oiling. Showing amazing dexterity, Marc pushed the sack over the crab's body and, lifting it up quickly, he pulled the string tightly and tied a knot, securing the sack. Returning to the Moke, he bundled the writhing mass under the seat where Laura was sitting. Both girls screamed!

"Land crab," Fidel told them nonchalantly as Marc started up the engine again.

"De make gud curry," said Marc.

Laura tried to keep her composure but the wriggling bundle kept touching the back of her legs and she was relieved when they arrived at Orient View. Grabbing their bags, she and Emma jumped out of the Moke at great speed.

"Come to the beach tonight," Marc called after them, "yuh can try du crab curry."

– – –

Blake's heart sank when Serena rang from New York to say she desperately needed some sun. He guessed her last-minute request to come to stay at the beach house was yet another ploy. There was no point in trying to talk her out of it on the phone. Their short relationship had recently fizzled out but Serena was determined to revive it. She was a young lady who didn't give up easily. By a stroke of manipulative genius, Serena had befriended his mother, Rhonda, who was now firmly in her corner, the result being a formidable tour de force. A pang of guilt told Blake he should have been tough, but it had been all too easy to just let Serena have her way, and of course it pleased his mother. But as her stay went on he wondered why he'd ever agreed to it. Serena was very demanding. Blake spent the day clothes shopping with her in Bridgetown. She'd spent the afternoon being pampered in the spa at Sandy Lane hotel. Serena was all about looking good. If dressing up and partying counted as work, then Serena would be a workaholic. She was not much of a conversationalist and he doubted she'd ever read a book. But she had a certain playful charm and to his shame he knew she looked good on his arm.

Blake had hoped to show her the reef or take her swimming in the beautiful calm waters of the Caribbean – not a chance. Serena said the breeze from the boat knotted her hair and she didn't like getting her hair wet. The few times she deigned to go into the pool she swam with her long blonde hair in a big shower cap, keeping her head well above water. These things used to make him smile; now they irritated him. He wondered if she would ever break out of her self-absorbed bubble. Blake sometimes had the urge to throw her playfully into the pool, but he always thought better of it. Anyway, she was leaving tomorrow and he didn't want any aggro tonight.

Blake's housekeeper, Myrtle, spent the afternoon preparing a meal for two and setting up the terrace. Blake enjoyed watching the sunset. He loved the way the colours changed and when darkness fell, he marvelled at how sudden it was. It was beautiful. When he was flying he had a unique viewpoint, unobstructed views to some of nature's most incredible sights: lightning, pink lakes, sunrise. In spite of this, his favourite place was sitting on his terrace watching the sun go down over the sea. Tonight, he hoped Serena would enjoy sharing the experience. He knew she would appreciate it more if food and champagne were involved.

Blake was waiting on the terrace with a beer when Serena arrived to join him. She looked beautiful, he had to admit. The blue dress she'd bought hugged her body in all the right places and the colour brought out the blue of her eyes.

"Oooh, champagne," she cooed, sitting down beside him. "It's been so good to be with you in the sunshine," she said, taking a sip.

"Glad you've enjoyed yourself," Blake replied, trying not to sound too disinterested.

"I can't wait to come again."

Blake felt the need to step up quickly.

"The truth is, Serena, I can't do this again. I'm tied with the business."

Besides, he'd met Laura! She was beautiful and he was looking forward to wooing her. Why couldn't Serena accept that it was over between them? He felt he'd made it clear enough, polite and to the point. Serena ignored his remark. It obviously wasn't what she wanted to hear. Selective hearing, he mused.

"I'm meeting Rhonda on Wednesday," she said. "We're going to the Plaza for lunch."

Blake heaved a sigh. So the waters were muddied. Serena was meeting his mother. Rhonda would want news. How did it go? Are you back together? This whole charade was making him feel trapped.

– – –

As the sun set, darkness fell, suddenly heralding the sights and sounds of a tropical evening. Laura found the lively chirping of the tree frogs comforting, and the flashes of light from the fireflies were a marvel to behold. They had decided to take up Marc's offer of crab curry. Laura had never been on the beach at night and she wasn't sure what to expect. As she descended the steps from her veranda, Emma came out of her apartment to greet her, accompanied by a young Bajan man dressed in khaki shorts and a white T-shirt. His smiling, amber eyes were beaming with pleasure as he stretched out his hand in a friendly hello.

"I'm Ivan," he said. "Hello, Laura."

Emma had spoken at length about her boyfriend, Ivan, during their outing earlier that day, but Laura had never met him until now. She liked him immediately. She knew he had grown up in Barbados and was a doctor at the local hospital.

"We've brought beers," he said, picking up a cooler box.

"I've brought white wine," replied Laura, holding up a bottle.

It was a beautiful, warm evening – the moon took on the appearance of a small cloud in the sky, surrounded by a multitude of stars. In the gardens along the beach, the magnificent breadfruit trees, which gave such welcome shade during the day, by night cast long shadows across the sand, giving the scene a dreamlike quality.

"I hear you walked into Bridgetown today, how was it?" asked Ivan.

"Just as I imagined," laughed Laura, "hot and busy."

The beach here was quiet, thankfully not in a tourist area. Most tourists stayed around the strip at St. Lawrence Gap. This, by contrast, was a working beach where the local fisherman kept their boats and mended their nets. They set sail around 5am each morning for the day's fishing and returned midday to sort the catch and deliver it to the fish market. Most went home before evening but a few stayed to relax and drink rum, the older men often playing a board game with seeds called "Warri". Played on a long wooden tray with twelve hollows and four seeds in each, the object of the game was to win the twenty-four seeds from your opponent. Emma explained that it was one of the oldest games in the world.

Approaching the back of the fish market, Laura could hear voices laughing and chatting and saw several shadowy figures sitting on deckchairs gathered around a fire burning in a brazier. On top of the embers was a big black pot. For Laura, there was something reassuring in the sight of a fire, a black pot and the smell of food. She was reminded of the black range in her grandmother's kitchen when she was growing up, with a kettle always on the go and a pot of food cooking to one side. Marc stood up to welcome them, his smile turning to laughter as Ivan handed over the cooler of beers. At the same time, a young girl aged about seven years old came running out of the fish market, her slight frame covered in a white dress, her long black curly hair hanging in two bunches down to her shoulders. She looked delighted to see them and, taking Emma's hand, she showed her to a small chair on the sand.

"Hello, Dulcie," said Emma, "have you been waiting for us?"

Fidel looked up expectantly, smiling his hello as they sat down on the deckchairs provided for them. Just then, Marc's wife, a large, cheery lady, emerged from the kitchen of the market carrying a tray which she then unloaded onto a table. It was full of cooked fish, pink plates, and an ice bucket. She threw her head back and laughed gleefully.

"Cheese-on-bread," she drawled, "yuh came."

"Hi, Aylen," said Emma. "Meet my friend, Laura. Of course we came, who can resist your crab curry?"

"Pass de fish round, Dulcie, give Laura sum," ordered Aylen.

Dutifully, Dulcie picked up the tray, now minus the ice bucket, and offered fish to their guests. The fish were elaborately displayed, with their tails in their mouths making a circular shape.

"Flying fish," said Ivan. "Delicious, and traditionally presented this way."

"Thanks, Dulcie," said Laura, taking one and putting it on her plate. Marc was busy handing the beers around. He uncorked the wine and poured a glass for Laura before putting the bottle in the ice bucket.

"Pass dat round, Dulcie," called Aylen from inside the market.

Picking up a smaller tray, Dulcie pressed Laura to take a chunk of fish from it, which she did gladly. Laura noticed Marc lean over towards Fidel, laughing and nodding in her direction. Fidel now looked at Laura as if apologising and then, as Marc spoke in his ear, a ray of light shone from his eyes and an impish grin lit up the old man's face. Shaking his head, he continued to smile. The others had noticed and were all looking at Laura. Self-consciously, she ate her fish, saying again how tasty it was. Aylen had now re-joined them and, lifting up her apron, laughed into it.

"Cheese-on-bread, didn't yuh tell the girl, Dulcie?"

"Tell me what?" asked Laura, looking around at the amused faces.

"She don't know what she eating." Marc was still laughing.

Laura was completely at a loss and went to take another piece of the chunky fish when Emma started to move her hand expressively in the air and mimicked the theme from *Jaws*. They all fell about laughing.

"You mean," Laura began as the penny dropped, "do you mean it's shark meat?"

"Yes," they all chorused.

Laura looked amazed and dismayed all at once.

"No bones in shark and it's dun well!" Marc was trying to placate her.

"I've never eaten shark before."

"First time for everything," said Emma, still laughing.

Laura began to relax and laugh at herself. "But it's lovely," she said, taking another piece, to which Aylen shrieked with laughter, pulling her apron over her face.

"Don't forget du crab curry," she called from behind, wiping her eyes.

This is pretty special, Laura thought, *eating out under the stars round a fire.* A lovely atmosphere had been generated by the simple pleasure of eating and drinking with friends. She began to feel like part of a community.

The full day had left Laura feeling very tired. It was almost midnight before she went to bed but was unable to sleep – her mind was such a jungle of thoughts. Late in the night, it was still hot as she made her way out onto the veranda, where it was only slightly cooler but enough to make her feel more comfortable. A half-moon was lighting the evening and she sat gazing at the sea for a long time. Her thoughts returned to Holy Island and her grandmother. Such introspective moments could come at any time and her mind clouded with sadness. She couldn't remember living in Barbados as a child. Part of her was still hurt that so many memories of her childhood had been kept from her. Perhaps it had all been too painful for her grandmother. Whatever the truth, she would never know. When her grandmother died, it was as if a link in a chain had broken and she was adrift. It was as though, until that moment, she had been sleepwalking through life, unquestioning, accepting. Suddenly, she felt differently about everything.

Casting her mind back to the way things were left between herself and David made her feel sad. They had been best friends for years. It all came to a head when he was down on one knee and the realisation sunk in: she didn't love him. She couldn't forget that look of hurt in his eyes. Ever since that day, a shroud of guilt had hung over her. David had always been there for her but she couldn't love him in the way he wanted.

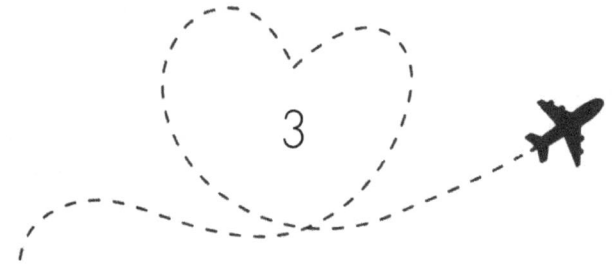

3

The days that followed Laura's foray into Bridgetown were quite tranquil. When Liam and Erika MacIver arrived back in Barbados, they invited her to come for an informal meeting at St. Catherine's before term began. Erika MacIver was head of St. Catherine's and her husband Liam was the school chaplain. The school was within walking distance and Emma accompanied her.

"There is so much to do – sort books, visual aids, timetables, rearrange my classroom… the list is endless!" Emma was animated.

"I'm really looking forward to it all. Teaching Key Stage 4 English Literature should be interesting, to say the least!" replied Laura. "Nothing like teenagers to keep you on your toes."

"You'll love it, Laura, I'm sure. The staff are so professional and Erika is so passionate about the school."

Laura knew education in Barbados was of a high standard; she had read extensively in preparation. St. Catherine's was an international school, offering CSEC as well as the UK national curriculum to those who required it, such as children of overseas workers who needed continuity of education whilst their parents were on contract in Barbados. Local parents sent their children there if they wished to prepare them for higher education abroad, thus making for a diverse selection of youngsters. The challenge of preparing years 10 and 11 for their exams was just what she needed. She hoped to meet new friends and colleagues and immerse herself in a completely different environment. Eight months' teaching at St. Catherine's would be perfect, she hoped.

In the cool of the morning, they were able to walk at a good pace as they turned into the narrow lanes off Bay Street and into the open countryside on the outskirts of St. Michael's district. They soon arrived at the large, black wrought-iron gates of the school. These gates were flanked by two lodges, one of which was occupied by the porter, who gave them a cheery wave as they passed through. Walking for about thirty metres between two rows of huge king palms, they came to a lemon-coloured building of considerable size. It was surrounded by a terrace, which formed a private garden in front and was accessible by several low, broad steps. The grandeur of the building took Laura by surprise.

As they slowly ascended the steps, a middle-aged man with laughing eyes and stooping shoulders came out of the entrance to greet them, smiling broadly.

"A sight for sore eyes," he exclaimed in a lilting Irish accent. "Liam."

He introduced himself to Laura, shaking her hand cordially, his left hand directing them through the doorway.

Inside the hallway was a hive of activity, with people milling around, talking, or passing through carrying books and papers. Emma took her leave and Liam showed Laura into a large drawing room, which she guessed was a staff room. It was comfortably arranged with sofas and chairs and coffee tables. There were several pictures on the walls: school photographs showing graduating students, teams of young students holding up winners' cups, and some of the school grounds. Laura glanced at them all with interest.

"Come and sit, Laura." Liam nodded towards a sofa, then called to a young woman. "Could you tell Erika that Laura's here, please? How's the apartment?" he asked.

"Lovely, thank you," she replied, amused at the speed of questioning.

"And Blake? He met you at the airport? No hiccups there? We gave him the small passport photo you sent us with your application."

"No hiccups," repeated Laura.

"It was very good of him. He was flying in from New York around the same time. He's a friend of our son, Charlie. In fact, Charlie works for him as a pilot."

Laura was surprised to hear that Charlie worked for Blake. *Interesting*, she thought.

Within minutes, an elegant lady in her fifties entered the room. Her attractive features showed her to be of Caribbean descent; her thick, black hair was tied back in a neat chignon. She wore a floral dress and wedge sandals. Smiling warmly, she greeted Laura.

"Ah, Laura, I'm Erika. We are so pleased to see you.

We're in great need of your assistance. Judith had to leave at such short notice when her husband was transferred to Miami." Erika stopped for breath. "Would you like something to drink?" she asked.

"Water, please," Laura replied.

"Let me get it," Liam offered, getting up as Erika came towards them.

"How do you find Barbados? Are you settling in?" Erika asked, sitting down next to her.

Liam returned with a jug of water and glasses on a small tray, which he lowered onto a table before proceeding to pour each of them a glass.

"I see you did your degree and PGCE at Edinburgh," Erika began. "We are so fortunate to get a well-qualified teacher this far into the academic year. We are blessed."

"I'm very pleased to be here," Laura told her.

Without further ado, Erika plunged into the business of the day. "We must go through the English Literature syllabus for years 10 and 11 KS4 before next week. It's all fairly straightforward. I will have Judith's records sent over to you. Also, while you are here, we will get you to sign your contract. It's the usual contractual verbiage, no surprises. And that's about it for now."

A few scribbles of the pen and Laura's contract was completed.

"Any questions you have, we're all here to help. All that's left to do when you are ready is a tour of the school grounds and I'll show you your classroom."

Laura smiled to herself. She admired Erika's indomitable enthusiasm.

– – –

Charlie MacIver and his wife Monica had arrived at Blake's beach house. They had flown in from Trinidad to stay with Blake for a few days.

Charlie had first met Blake when they both worked as pilots for American Airlines. Charlie joined Blake at Cargo Air when he first set up the company. They began the enterprise with two fixed-wing planes, which were economical on fuel, ideal for small airports and offered a fast turnaround. They initially serviced a niche in the market and the business had grown exponentially. They now had three planes and four pilots, as well as a warehouse and office staff. Trinidad was now their hub airport and Charlie had moved there to take charge of operations. Blake owned and financed the company. He wanted to expand quickly – a company must keep moving forward, Blake knew that. Blake was the strategist and negotiator. They were a successful partnership and best friends to boot.

Charlie and Monica had come to Barbados to see Charlie's parents but also to celebrate with Blake. The company had recently acquired a B757-200 aircraft to extend their freight capacity. The plane was to be fitted with pallet wheels for cargo. Blake would pick up the plane in New York in a month or so and fly it to Trinidad.

Over coffee in the kitchen, the friends caught up with the latest news.

"How was the long weekend with Serena?" Charlie asked.

"Long," replied Blake. "She enjoyed herself before heading back to a freezing New York."

It was a terse response and it was all Blake was prepared to say. Charlie didn't pursue the matter. Trying to discuss Blake's private life in any detail would cross the forbidden line – it was off limits.

"Let's celebrate somewhere tomorrow night," Blake said spontaneously, changing the subject. "Monica, you choose."

"I love the restaurant in Bathsheba," she suggested, "but I can't think of the name."

"Cliffside," said Blake.

"That's it," she smiled.

"I'll arrange it and get Rudy to drive us. I'm thinking of asking a friend along, is that okay?" Blake added furtively.

Charlie looked directly at Blake in surprise. "Of course, male or female?" Charlie asked, having already guessed the answer from Blake's demeanour, but he was fishing anyway.

"Female, someone I met recently." Blake was still not forthcoming. "Wait and see. If all goes to plan, you'll meet her tomorrow."

Charlie and Monica exchanged glances and shrugged. Blake never invited anyone unless it was business, and tomorrow night was not. Charlie was keen to know more. He considered for a moment and then decided not to ask. They would find out soon enough.

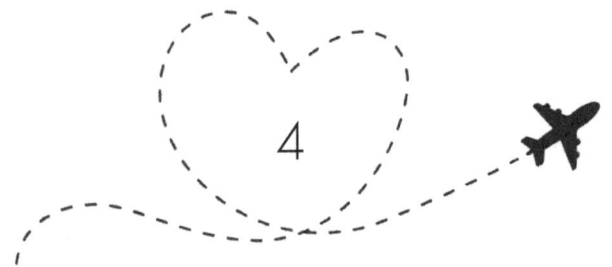

4

Laura was on a high when she arrived back at Orient View. The school visit had gone well. She had really warmed to Erika and Liam and couldn't wait to get started.

The heat of the day had been oppressive and the now cooler evening offered a much welcome relief. Laura had still not quite acclimatised. Emma was joining her on the balcony later. They had started to get together at dusk with a cool drink, to relax and discuss the curiosities of life in Barbados. From their vantage point on the veranda they had a panoramic view of the bay. As the sun rapidly neared the horizon, it alternately lit up the ocean or threw into shadow the boats and trees along the beach. Then, just as it sunk below the skyline, a vapoury green line displayed its brightness for a few seconds as night fell. It was known as the 'green flash' – Marc had told them about this phenomenon. They had managed to catch sight of it once but usually they were distracted at the last moment.

Tonight, Emma had hoped to hear feedback from

Laura's first visit to St. Catherine's but it would have to wait. Ivan, who had asked if he could join them for a welcome beer after he finished at the hospital, had brought his father Marvin along. Laura hadn't met Marvin before but found him to be good company. He was a stocky Bajan, charming and witty. He lectured in Business at Cave Hill University. His Irish wife, Carmel, was a flight attendant with Aer Lingus when they met over thirty years ago. They had been together ever since. Ivan was their only son. Marvin, it seemed, always had something to be animated about, waving his arms in the air or running his hands through his black, curly hair. Laura had learnt that in his youth Marvin had been a well-known Calypso singer. He was certainly never short of words, and Laura found it easy to imagine him with a guitar slung around his neck. The four of them were enjoying the evening air and a few drinks. Marvin had launched full sail into his topic for tonight.

"Today, Barbados is one of the most developed countries in the Eastern Caribbean, but it wasn't always so…" He was cut short by the unexpected arrival of Blake who, on seeing that Laura had visitors, apologised brusquely for interrupting their evening and turned to leave. Remembering how she felt when she had seen him in Bridgetown with another woman, Laura felt inclined at first to let him go. However, not one for holding grudges, she called him back to join them. Ivan handed him a beer. Laura noticed Emma giving her a secretive look and smiling.

Marvin had allowed himself a brief pause, but as it was

never easy for him to leave his subject half finished, he continued pompously, "As I was saying, for many years the economy of Barbados was totally dependent on rum and sugar cane. And that was not so long ago. When the West Indies Federation collapsed, we became a Commonwealth realm."

Although she heard words, Laura's mind was too full of Blake's presence. She glanced over to him and Blake smiled at her and winked, a hint of mischief in his eyes. In spite of herself, she found him so attractive, and the charm of the evening had gone up a notch for her. Marvin was still in full flow.

"At that time, the CDC aimed to finance and develop a more diverse economy such as tourism, financial services and some manufacturing, as part of the Government Plan."

On hearing CDC, something clicked in Laura's memory: a letterhead, something she had seen in the box of papers and photos her grandmother had given her.

"Is CDC the same as the 'Commonwealth Development Corporation'?" she asked.

It was a moment of impulse.

"It is," said Marvin. "Have you heard of them, Laura?"

Laura hesitated, at first wishing she had kept quiet, knowing that she was about to reveal something she had only recently learnt herself, but she decided to continue.

"My father was a land surveyor. He came to Barbados to work for the CDC."

As soon as she'd said it, she wanted to take it back. She was usually a very private person. The revelation was met with surprise. Ivan was first to speak.

"Okay, Dad, lecture over."

Laura hadn't imagined her comment would stop them in their tracks, but it was too late; they were waiting expectantly for her to elaborate.

"I don't know much," she said honestly. "Just that my father worked for the CDC and that I lived in Barbados for three years. I came when I was six months old. That's it really."

Laura looked around at the faces before her. She had their full attention, and it made her feel uncomfortable. Emma was incredulous.

"That's amazing, where did you live, Laura?"

"Paradise Heights. I have a photo of me with my parents, taken in the garden there."

"And where do they live now?" Marvin wondered.

"They died in a car accident in Edinburgh when I was three years old. They were on a short visit back to the UK."

"Very sad." Blake was the first to speak softly.

The others nodded silently.

It was the first time she had opened up about her parents.

"I live in Paradise Heights, it's up near the university. What were their names, Laura?" Marvin asked.

"My father was John and my mother was Rose."

Marvin sat back in his seat and exhaled slowly.

"I vaguely remember that a family went on holiday and didn't return. Carmel and I hadn't lived there long and we thought nothing of it, contracts change, people move on…"

Marvin's words trailed off as he now dwelt on what had really happened.

"Oh my, Laura," he continued. "You were the little girl I would see going shopping with your mother or setting off in the car with your parents at the weekend."

"Probably," said Laura. Her heart began to beat quickly at the realisation that Marvin may well have seen her as child. "Because often, on Sundays, my parents met friends at the Abbeyville for lunch and they would take me swimming in the pool. Apparently, my mother loved the banana daquiris there."

"Yes, in its heyday, the Abbeyville was known for its banana daquiris. I've enjoyed a few there myself," Marvin grinned.

"How do you know all this?" Ivan asked.

"Letters and cards from my mother to my grandmother."

"Memories, precious memories." Marvin spoke reflectively, shaking his head.

Such moments of coincidence can come when you least expect them, and this was one such moment for both Laura and Marvin. Laura went to her bedroom and returned with her precious photograph.

"That frame is gorgeous, Laura. Did you make it?" Emma asked.

"Yes. I love to collect shells and things from the beach and give them new life. I saw this piece of driftwood. It looked like it had had a long, hard journey in the sea so I picked it up. I felt it would make the perfect frame for my parents' photograph. This photo in the garden is the only one I have of me with both of my parents."

Marvin studied it carefully.

"I know the house and the owner," he said. "Would you like to see it again?"

"Yes, I would, in time."

"Sometimes it can help to look at the past," said Marvin kindly.

The matter was dropped but before he left Marvin announced quietly to Laura that he would speak to the owner in Paradise Heights.

Blake had been quiet for most of the evening but now, alone with Laura, he seemed in a reflective frame of mind.

"Sorry to hear about your parents," he said.

"The moment felt right, somehow, to talk about them," she said. The moment had in fact felt cathartic for Laura.

Blake turned to leave but hesitated. "I actually called, Laura, to ask you if you would like to join me with friends tomorrow night, in a small celebration?"

Laura looked at him quizzically.

"What sort of celebration?" she asked.

"Business." His reply was brief. "We're going to a restaurant on the other side of the island. I think you'll enjoy it."

Laura thought for a moment. She seemed preoccupied – Blake understood.

"What time were you thinking of going?"

"We can pick you up around 6 p.m."

Laura gave a casual nod 'okay'. Blake felt a tightness in his chest, as he did after a hard business negotiation.

"Hey, I've brought you some new shades," he said, delving into the pocket of his shorts.

"No need, I bought some more at the little supermarket next door, but thank you, Blake, that's very thoughtful."

Laura looked up in surprise as he handed her a black pouch.

"Oh, they're Ray-Bans."

"Are there any other kind?" he teased.

"Well, mine were budget's finest," she replied.

He smiled. Laura, with the long, dark hair and big, blue eyes, had captivated him. She was beautiful and smart and, most of all, she had no agenda. She was someone he wanted to get to know, but he knew he would have to play his cards right. He gave her a polite kiss on the cheek.

"If you decide to go to Paradise Heights, I'll take you," he said kindly.

Laura didn't argue.

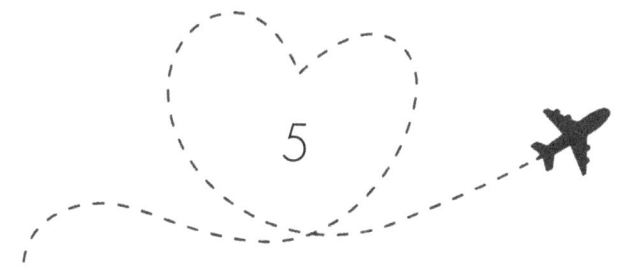

5

Laura took a warm shower and washed her hair with her frothy strawberry shampoo, rinsing it well. She left it to dry naturally. So, what should she wear? Searching her limited wardrobe, she discarded her little black number – it wasn't a date! Laura had accepted Blake's invitation at face value: to accompany him to a business celebration. *Straightforward enough*, she told herself. She chose a long, turquoise, strappy dress, sandals and silver earrings. Pulling her damp hair to one side, she let it fall over her shoulder. She felt cool and comfortable.

Blake arrived promptly at six and came up to the open veranda door. He was wearing a white, formal shirt and light grey trousers, his shirt sleeves slightly rolled up, his Rolex Oyster Daytona shining against his tanned arm. Her heart jumped a little, he looked so devastatingly handsome. He leaned to kiss her on the cheek and she caught the exotic aroma of expensive cologne.

"You look beautiful," he said.

Such a charmer, she thought.

Opening the door of the Merc, Blake helped Laura slip into the back seat next to Monica and Charlie, who greeted her warmly and with some interest. Blake got into the front next to his driver, Rudy, and they set off.

The road to Bathsheba ran for about fifteen kilometres east from the bay along narrow roads between cane fields. Then, gradually widening, the road became enclosed by a chain of hills on each side as it twisted its way downwards and deep ravines and crevices threw mysterious shadows over the rocks. As they rounded the last curve in the road, the gorgeous views of the rugged coast spread before them, undulating into the distance and down to the sea. Before her was the most striking vista Laura had ever seen.

Rudy brought the car to a halt outside a small, unobtrusive building nestled between two sloping cliffs. The sounds of the crashing waves added drama to this melancholy landscape, which was almost invisible now in the increasing darkness. Laura was immediately reminded of home. Blake was out of the front seat and holding out a hand to assist Laura before she got her seat belt undone. *Blake*, she considered, *is nothing if not chivalrous*.

On leaving the car, Charlie and Monica hugged and kissed her in welcome. They seemed genuinely pleased to meet her. Blake put his arm protectively around her shoulders as they entered the building. They were greeted politely by the owner, Eugene, who obviously knew Blake. Eugene escorted them through a small reception room and onto a large terrace with sweeping views. Laura's eyes opened wide as she took it all in. Several tables were covered with white tablecloths and set for dinner, candlelight flickering from the centre of each one, giving an aura of tranquillity in marked contrast to the swirling waters of the Atlantic Ocean beneath. The elegant ambience signified a very exclusive restaurant.

There was a moment or two of embarrassed silence as they were first seated. Charlie and Monica looked at her inquisitively. Laura smiled politely and took a lingering look at her dinner companions as Blake ordered champagne.

Monica was stunning. Her dark eyes lit up her face, and her long, black hair was tied back in a braided ponytail. She wore a black and gold kaftan set off by two large, gold earrings which sparkled in the candlelight as she moved her head. Charlie was equally attractive. His playful blue eyes were the first thing she noticed – they shone with warmth and openness – and his tall frame and powerful shoulders, evidence he was no stranger to the gym.

This could be fun. This was not the business celebration she had imagined.

Blake sat down beside Laura, having spoken to the maître d'. who moments later returned with a bottle of Dom Perignon in an ice bucket and ceremoniously poured champagne into four tulip glasses. Leaving the bottle in the ice bucket on a stand beside their table, he left discreetly. Charlie was first to lift his glass to propose a toast.

"To continued success."

"To good friends," Blake added.

The evening was beginning to feel unreal for Laura. The bubbles of champagne felt cool in her mouth and she began to feel comfortable. A second glass of champagne and Laura felt relaxed, even a little lightheaded as she hadn't eaten. Blake too seemed to have lost some of the tension he usually had. As he looked at her, Laura noticed his deep brown eyes had a dreamy quality.

"This is my favourite part of Barbados; it's wild and untamed. This area you see around us is called Scotland. I love it here," he said.

In only a few short weeks, her own island now seemed so far away, like a distant memory, and she felt a momentary pang of homesickness. "I grew up on a small island close to Scotland called Holy Island."

Blake gave her a steady, searching look. "Well, I'm damned," he exclaimed, "I've never heard of it."

Charlie had heard of it.

"In the RAF, we did low-flying exercises over the Cheviot Hills because Northumberland is so sparsely populated. Holy Island is around that area, isn't it, Laura?"

"We are actually in Berwick on the Scottish border. The Island has a three-mile causeway from the mainland, the first part of which is completely under the North Sea. You can cross at low tide but you must be careful or you could be swept out to sea. Crossing time is given daily by the coastguard."

"I've heard," Charlie mused, "that some people try to beat the tide and end up having to climb onto escape towers before their cars become completely submerged or taken out to sea."

"Outrageous!" said Monica in amazement.

"Is that name for real? Holy Island?" asked Blake.

"The actual name is the Holy Island of Lindisfarne. It was settled by a monk called St. Aidan in the seventh century but everyone knows it as Holy Island."

Laura was hoping they would leave it at that – she didn't want to dwell on the memory, it made her feel sad.

"The very idea of a Holy Island," Blake smiled in amusement. "Awesome."

"Check it out, Blake," said Charlie, laughing.

At that moment Eugene brought menus to the table. He asked if they would like suggestions or alternatively if they wished to request something that was not on the menu, the chef would do his best to oblige. He then left them to mull through their choices.

"Now, will you permit me to give some advice on the menu?" Monica jumped in.

"Works for me," said Blake, "how about you, Laura?"

"Not being au fait with Caribbean cuisine – well, apart from the roti – I'm more than happy for Monica to select for me," she replied.

Looking delighted, Monica carried on reading aloud. "As you see, there is couscous with pan-fried flying fish, the national dish of Barbados. You must try it. The conkies here are the best on the island – sweet potato, grated coconut, raisins, all wrapped and steamed in banana leaves. There's pickled pork, fresh salad, raw and pickled salad. We'll share a selection and a duo of blackbelly lamb for main."

The meal planned, she looked up to see Charlie smiling and Blake and Laura looking shell-shocked.

"Go for it," said Blake. "Are you cool with that, Laura?"

"I'm fine," she replied. In truth, she had no idea what to expect.

"I'll explain each dish when it arrives," Monica promised, giving their order to Eugene.

Blake ordered more champagne.

"Remember, we're here to celebrate."

"What are we celebrating exactly?" Laura asked.

"A good year for the company," Blake replied, sounding almost brusque, Laura felt.

"And expansion," added Monica. "Don't forget that! They have invested in a new plane, Laura."

Monica's voice bubbled with excitement. Laura noticed for the first time that Blake looked a little uncomfortable, as if he wanted to change the subject. Charlie did it for him.

"What brought you to Barbados, Laura?"

"When my grandmother died recently, I discovered that as a very young child I had lived in Barbados."

"You didn't know this before?" he asked.

"No, my parents died in a car crash on a visit to the UK. My grandmother never spoke about it the entire time I lived with her. My mother, Rose, was her only daughter, I think it upset her too much. I came to Barbados out of curiosity for my past. I wanted some connection."

"That makes sense," said Charlie.

"Your turn, Blake," said Monica pointedly. "I wonder why you left New York to make your home in Barbados?"

Blake had been noticeably quiet, but Laura's instinct told her there was something to find out.

"We're all interested," Charlie added, playing devil's advocate.

"Okay, here's the thing," Blake began good-humouredly, "I never felt I belonged in New York. I realised I was measuring everything with money and I had lost myself."

Laura was astonished, she hadn't expected that. All eyes were now on Blake.

"Care to elaborate?" asked Charlie. "I mean, we cannot live without money, that's the system."

"Oh I value money as much as the next person, but I value my independence more. I just didn't want to…" Blake paused.

"To be defined by money?" queried Laura.

"Exactly," he replied. "My father owns a property empire in New York which has been in the family for generations. It consumes his every waking moment and I don't want to be part of it. After Harvard and the air force I never went back home. I came to Barbados and started my own small air cargo with a legacy left to me by my grandfather. My parents were furious. They still consider me a maverick."

"Would you say you are running away from family, Blake?" Laura was curious.

"Not at all. Moving away is not the same thing. My life is here, it is my choice."

"Good for you, Blake, but are you trying to leave your past behind?" Monica asked. "Sorry, that is personal," she quickly retracted.

"That's okay. No, the past is always part of you, that's just how it is." Blake paused to look at Laura. "Your past, Laura, brought you to Barbados."

The conversation was getting heavy, but the others didn't seem to mind; they were old friends. For Laura, the night had given her a new insight into Blake Degas. Their backgrounds, however, could not be more different. Blake was from a wealthy family – she was not. Laura admired his strong, independent values. The night was beautiful and Laura didn't want it to end. For the first time in ages, she felt… happy.

On their return to Orient View, Laura bid farewell to Charlie and Monica as Blake accompanied her to the veranda steps.

"Thank you for a lovely evening," she said.

Blake moved closer to her.

Laura felt herself blush under the intensity of his gaze.

"My pleasure," he said huskily.

"Please, Blake," she said, dropping her head.

"I understand," he replied. "I'd better go."

But he was reluctant to leave. Laura wasn't responding to his advances in the way he expected. He realised he would have to up his game.

"It's Trinidad Carnival in a few weeks. How about I take you down there? We can catch up with Charlie and Monica."

The invitation was impulsive. As a rule, he was never impulsive, but Laura was doing strange things to his psyche.

Jeez, Laura mused, *Blake doesn't hang about.*

"I'm surprised to hear you ask that," she said. "I thought you'd be busy."

Blake had surprised himself but there it was, he'd said it and he meant it.

"Everyone takes time out for Carnival," he said lightly.

"My offer stands. Think about it."

Laura laughed softly. She was tempted, but she needed ground rules.

"Blake, at some point I need to talk to you," she said quickly. It sounded feeble, she knew.

"Sure, any time after next week." His dark eyes looked slightly bewildered, wondering what Laura might have to say to him.

"Well, in that case," Laura spoke slowly, "why don't I cook for you a week on Saturday? It won't be fine dining; I'll cook something from Holy Island's cuisine," she smiled. "We can discuss Trinidad."

"Fine by me," he said, "I'll bring wine."

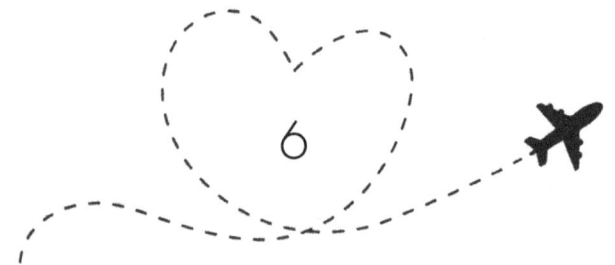

6

This was the second night Laura had passed at home marking essays from Year Eleven, asking for their thoughts on the relationship between Romeo and Juliet. The group discussion in class had proven promising. A few students were quite outspoken. Anton was first to offer his particular point of view.

"Romeo's such a loser," he had said.

"Why, because he fell in love?" Alvita was amazed.

"Yeah, because one day it's Rosalind, the next day Juliet."

It was a good point, Laura thought.

"What about the intense passion between Romeo and Juliet?" Clara asked.

"I didn't like the sound of it," scoffed Anton.

Laura almost laughed out loud.

"We're talking about the greatest love story ever told," Alvita said indignantly.

"Yeah," said Emilio. "Look how that went down."

Laura smiled to herself. She had been looking

forward to their written follow-up. But each paper was disappointingly like an echo of the last. Laura knew many of her students had a powerful, even overactive imagination, and some were better than others at creating stories. Yet when it came to course work, they all regurgitated traditional views, which made for tedious reading.

She must work on their confidence to develop real opinions and to present them in an appropriate way, to encourage them to read around the topics more widely.

St. Catherine's had an excellent library for textbooks, but was a little short on fiction, poetry and books that could open up new perspectives on the same subject. If only the school library could include a wider selection – but she knew budgets were tight.

"Hi, can I come in?" Emma appeared in the doorway waving a piece of paper. "I wanted to show you Dulcie's poem."

Laura looked up as Emma handed her the paper, glad of the interruption.

ME THINK

ME THINK toothbrushes grow on trees
Honey cake made by bees BUT ME WRONG
ME THINK birds can go to the moon
Helicopters only come out at noon BUT ME WRONG
ME THINK butterflies come from the sky
Jasmine can fly way up high BUT ME WRONG
ME THINK parents don't know a thing
Fees make my head spin BUT ME WRONG
ME THINK fishes can't swim
Sun makes the world dim BUT ME WRONG

"It's marvellous, Emma, so refreshing to read. For a seven-year-old, Dulcie has a unique way with words."

"I know, and she loves poetry. She tells me you lent her a poetry book."

Laura nodded. "I have another one for her, *Caribbean Poems*. The one I lent her has a story to it."

"I'd like to hear that," said Emma.

"Well, as a child I loved books. My world was so small that a trip across the causeway to Alnwick was a big deal for me. My grandmother would take me to a quirky bookshop housed in an old train station. On opening the doors we entered an Aladdin's cave of books. They had every kind imaginable, old and new, on tables and shelves. There were open fires, sofas, armchairs, and a miniature train circled on a track above your head. I was allowed to browse through the children's section. Then we would have tea and an iced bun in their café in what was the old waiting room. When I left I was usually clutching at least three second-hand books that my grandmother had bought for me. They meant the world to me," Laura sighed.

"That's a lovely memory," said Emma.

"I don't suppose I could keep this, could I, Emma? I'd like to frame it for Dulcie."

"Please do, she'll be thrilled, it will encourage her. Pity we don't have a library for lower school. What a boon that would be, to have our own selection of poetry books," said Emma.

Laura smiled, "I was thinking that very thing."

Emma warmed to the theme. "I would love to see story books, poetry books, picture books, all sorts of books, in an ideal world. We have a bookcase in our classrooms and

that's fine for simple readers, but a well-stocked library...
what an asset," she said.

Laura considered for a moment. "I might have a word with Erika, fancy coming with me? See if there's any extra money in the kitty."

"Sure," said Emma. "If it's good for St. Catherine's, Erika will do her level best to make it happen."

"I know she will, I'm banking on it," said Laura.

"Anyone in?" Ivan called.

Laura looked round.

"Come in, we're just talking shop. Well, libraries, actually – how important they are."

"You know Barbados opened the first free public library outside of the UK and America in 1906. That's why we have such a high literacy rate," he said.

"No." They both shook their heads.

"We're talking school library," said Laura.

"Oh right," said Ivan. "Well, that aside, have you eaten?" he asked.

"I'm starving," said Emma.

Laura also felt in need of sustenance. She hadn't eaten since breakfast; she had been so keen to get through the marking. There wasn't much in her fridge either – a bowl of salad and a shrivelled tomato. She must shop tomorrow, she thought.

"Only if we go Dutch," she said.

"No way, Laura, we had supper here last week, this is my treat." Ivan dismissed her offer.

"Are you sure?" Laura asked.

"No argument," he replied.

"Okay, thanks, Ivan. I'll just wash my hands and put a brush through my hair, two ticks," she said.

"How about we go for a roti?" he added.

"Now you're talking," said Emma and Laura in unison. They didn't need asking twice.

They wandered along to the Roti Hut, a small take-away-cum-café along Bay Street about fifteen minutes away. The air was warm and heavy and still, even by Bajan standards, and the walk very pleasant. They stopped outside a ramshackle building huddled by the side of the road in the shadows. Laura looked up; she had never noticed it before, it had a certain charm, she thought, even in disrepair. A young man greeted them, and with a flourish of the arm directed them towards the back. Beaming at Laura and Emma, he grabbed Ivan's hand, shaking it vigorously and nudging his elbow.

"Hi, Doc, wa gine how's de fiddle?" he asked, winking at Ivan.

"Good to see you," Ivan replied cautiously, looking uncomfortable.

Then something happened that amused Laura. What started out as an ordinary handshake and a cheeky nudge, unfortunately somehow went wrong. Their arms seemed to take on a life of their own. As the young man continued walking Ivan ended up with his arm behind his back, still being held by him. Thus, what hitherto had been a friendly gesture turned into a sort of arm-wrestle. In an attempt to recover his composure, Ivan wrenched his arm free and adjusted his shirt sleeve. He looked ruffled. Emma rolled her eyes.

The small courtyard was sufficiently surrounded by colourful plants in tubs, to prevent the sounds of the Bay Street traffic penetrating. There were only two tables, both covered with dark green, checked oilcloths. The trio sat down; they were the only ones there. Ordering three beers, they sat back to enjoy the evening air.

"Well, that was a real Tom and Jerry moment," Emma began. "What's all that about de fiddle?"

Ivan exhaled as if expecting the question. "Just a local greeting."

Emma cocked an eyebrow. "Really! What sort of greeting?" Emma liked to know details. Seeing no way out, Ivan cut straight to the chase.

"A *how's your love life* greeting, just banter between men," he said.

It suddenly got interesting for Emma. "Just banter? Meaning, basically, how's your sex life?" she asked.

Ivan squirmed. Laura winced in sympathy.

"Because you walked in with two women?" Emma was enjoying this.

"Two beautiful women." Ivan was quick, he was no fool. Laura suppressed a giggle. "You don't give an answer," he began again defensively.

"I should hope not." Emma feigned offence.

"It's like when you say, 'Hello, how are you?' We don't expect people to actually tell us. Although in my case," he shrugged, "they do expect me to respond to their list of ailments, so I don't ask."

The two girls laughed. Laura loved Ivan's droll sense of humour.

"Well, at least I've learnt something." Emma grinned. "I won't think of fiddles in the same way again."

The young waiter returned with their beers. "What yuh gonna eat?"

"Three chicken and okra rotis, please," Ivan ordered.

"A few minutes," he told them, with a rocking movement of his right hand.

Now, Laura did understand this. She had learnt that time could be pretty flexible in Barbados. A few minutes accompanied by the hand-rolling movement could mean anything up to a few hours. She was reminded of her one and only trip to a local hairdresser. "About 11 a.m.," the young girl had said with the hand rolling, so she arrived on time. The salon was lively, with laughter, gossip, even snacking – a real social occasion. Around 3 p.m. they had started on her hair! Laura learnt that this was quite usual – part of the laid-back charm of Barbados – but if you wanted your hair done on time, it was better to go to a tourist hotel.

Tonight, however, service was positively speedy, and the still-beaming waiter returned with their rotis in fifteen minutes. And they were divine, they told him as they finished up.

"Best on de island," he pronounced as he cleared away their plates. "Tell de chef." He gestured towards a large Bajan lady who came out smiling and red-faced from the kitchen to ask if they had eaten well. They were all impressed that 'de chef' turned out to be his seventy-year-old grandmother.

Emma glanced at her watch. "It's only 8.30 p.m., there's

loads of time – no work tomorrow," she sighed, reticent to end the night.

"I know where we'll go," said Ivan. "Are you ready?"

It was around nine by the time they'd reached the Reggae Shack: a bright red building with a huge wooden balcony, right on the beach close to Bridgetown. The hypnotic reggae bass beat greeted them as they approached. Going through the open door, they entered a room of randomly placed tables and chairs arranged around a stage at one end with organist, drummer, guitarist and bass player, and space in front of them for dancing. A long mahogany bar ran along one side of the room, with several tall bar stools arranged alongside the counter. The room was lit by an assortment of bulbs in hurricane lamps hanging from the ceiling, which was pleasantly high. It had a real late nightclub feel to it. The customers were made up of local businesspeople after work, smartly dressed couples and locals in casual clothes. *All life is here,* mused Laura as they sat down at a nearby table. There was a comfortably unreal atmosphere, a feeling of being separated from the rest of the world – detached from normal life – she loved it! The music was rhythmic and mellow, serenading all who came to enjoy the beer, the rum, and the entertainment.

The beer was sold in jugs. It didn't look like a red wine sort of place, so Laura and Emma asked for rum and Coke. Ivan returned from the bar carrying a jug of beer and two glasses, accompanied by a tall young man carrying two rum and Cokes.

"Guess who I found at the bar." Ivan nodded towards the young man.

"Sean, meet Emma and Laura. Sean is a doctor from Ireland who has just started at the hospital, last week in fact."

He motioned to Sean to sit down and join them.

"Good to meet you," Sean smiled at them. "I'm in digs at the hospital, so I haven't been out much. Someone recommended this place."

The fair-haired, handsome doctor appeared to be grateful for the company. Sean also turned out to have kissed the Blarney Stone and regaled them with hilarious tales of his first week in Barbados. Laura relaxed and immersed herself in the fun ambience of the evening.

A sudden chortling of merriment made them look across the room, where a group of young people were enjoying a get-together. A young girl was enticing a young man to get up to dance. She had managed to get the man onto his feet, to the amusement of the others. Putting her arms around his neck, she moved closer to him. He held his hands firmly on her hips, ensuring a polite distance between them. Undeterred, she leaned her head against his chest as they moved slowly to the music of Bob Marley's "Waiting in Vain". The poor guy couldn't have looked more uncomfortable; the young woman obviously had the hots for him and wanted to make sure he knew.

"Are you kidding?" Emma put her hand to her mouth, she hadn't meant the words to escape so loudly. The others followed her gaze through the dimly lit room. Laura did a double-take and cringed. The reluctant young man was Blake.

Laura almost felt sorry for Blake – he was too attractive by half, so many women wanted a piece of him. Laura felt sorry for the girl too, she'd been blatant about the way she went after Blake, a crush gone public. Laura watched as Blake slowly manoeuvred her back towards the group. Smiling good-naturedly, he pulled her arms from around his neck and helped her back into her seat as the others, still in high spirits, clapped and cheered. Blake chose this moment to come across the room to their table.

"If only I'd kept my mouth shut." Emma was apologetic for drawing attention to them. Laura was surprised Blake had recognised them in the dimness, but he had.

His hair looked slightly ruffled. Several buttons were open on his white shirt. Laura could see his chest muscles as he walked towards them.

Ivan greeted him warmly. "You seem to be having fun, Blake."

"And then some," said Blake, heaving a sigh. "Office staff. Marissa is twenty-one tomorrow. I took them for a meal after work and they wanted to come here. I feel obliged to hang around to see them all home safely."

They went through the motions of greeting each other. Laura tried to concentrate on keeping her expression calm, but her heart was pumping in her ears. Blake looked so gorgeous standing there and she hadn't expected to see him. Feeling ill at ease, she turned to Sean.

"Sean, meet Blake," she said.

The two men shook hands affably. Blake looked at Laura with questioning eyes. He arched an eyebrow. "What brings you all here?" he asked testily.

The question may have sounded casual, but Laura had the feeling it was a euphemism for "who's this guy?".

"Relaxing, no work tomorrow," Ivan answered, oblivious to any tension.

Blake was now staring at Laura; something was happening between them. Laura wasn't sure what it was. She tried to look away but their eyes locked for a moment. The colour rose in her cheeks.

Blake choked back his discomfort at seeing Laura with another man. He was feeling a tumult of emotion quite new to him. Laura looked beautiful, her skin glowed and her blue eyes sparkled. He had been aware of other men watching her with interest, especially this Sean. Yet he knew that whoever Laura was out with was none of his business. He took a deep breath. He couldn't think straight – he needed to get out of there. There was an awkward silence.

"Guess I'd better make tracks, get this lot home." He nodded towards the table still celebrating. "Enjoy your evening." And he was gone.

Every second of the encounter had been cringeworthy for Laura, and now suddenly it was over.

"He's so dreamy," said Emma, also oblivious.

Sean looked slightly bemused. "I half expected pistols at dawn for a moment." So, he had picked up on the tensity. "Are you two an item?" he asked Laura.

"No, of course not," she said diffidently.

She wondered if the attentions of his young member of staff had thrown Blake off balance, but no, she thought. If she didn't know better, she would have said Blake was jealous.

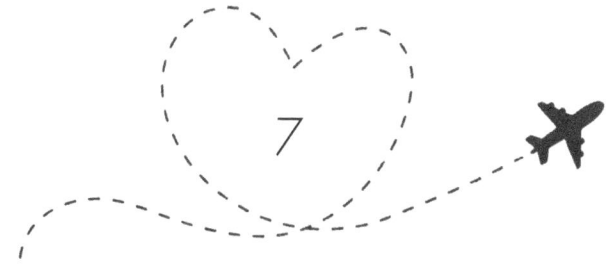

7

Close to noon on Saturday, Laura returned from the Star supermarket along Bay Street. Tonight, she was cooking for Blake and really looking forward to it – the cooking part anyway. There was rarely the opportunity for her to practise her culinary skills in Barbados. Her lunch was provided in school and in the evening fruit or salads were sufficient. On occasions, Aylen would invite Emma and herself to join the family on the beach for a fish barbecue. So all in all, there was not much call for cooking. The menu she had chosen was at least reminiscent of Holy Island cuisine, but obviously not quite the authentic replication. The evening was meant to be a bit of fun and a nod towards the tastes of her homeland. More importantly, it would provide the chance for her to have a private conversation with Blake and this she was not looking forward to. Blake had somehow gate-crashed her life and Laura was keen to establish boundaries. This was not going to be an easy discussion to have. She hoped the opportunity would arise over dinner for her to broach the matter delicately. These thoughts were eddying around in her mind. Laura anticipated the evening with mixed feelings.

There was a tap at the door – it was Aylen with a tray of oysters.

"Hope de gud," she said, handing them to Laura. "A gift from we." So saying, she turned and hurried down the steps, blowing kisses to Laura as she went.

"Thank you, Aylen, thank Marc for me, that's very kind," Laura called after her. Laura was touched by their generosity. She hoped they didn't think she was using them tonight as an aphrodisiac. *No, of course not*, she quickly dismissed the idea.

It was Laura's intention to make Lindisfarne Oysters for starters. They were unusual, she reasoned, inasmuch as they were served hot, with butter, gruyere cheese and fresh breadcrumbs, grilled and then sprinkled with parsley. Laura much preferred them to the raw, throw it to the back of your throat and taste the sea water oysters. She realised her preference came under the shaky realms of taste, and she knew she wasn't really that sophisticated. For main, Pan Haggerty, made with sliced potatoes, would accompany the rack of lamb. The "singing hinnies" dessert was similar to a griddle-scone-like mixture with added lemon, cream of tartar and dried fruits. From planning, to shopping, to now preparing the food, she was finding the entire process to be therapeutic.

Laura enjoyed Blake's company and she was pleased that in some small way she could return his generosity.

However, there was always that unwritten line between friendship and something more that she wasn't ready to cross – but she guessed Blake was. Laura had the feeling Blake was a bit of a player. She didn't know for sure whether he really liked her, or was she just the new girl in town? However, Blake was the first person she'd met in Barbados and this connection meant something to her. She wanted his friendship.

By late afternoon, the preparation was done. The air was warm and heavy and very still. The heat of the day could be felt emanating from the walls and Laura opened the windows to let in what little moving air there was. She began to set the table for two, having found a white cloth and burgundy place mats and napkins in a kitchen drawer. After adding cutlery and glasses, she thought that the table looked inviting. Not wishing to suggest a romantic dinner, she declined from putting a candle in the centre, instead choosing to turn on the floor lamp that stood beside the potted palm in the corner. This threw light between the leaves, casting interesting shadows and patterns onto the ceiling and walls.

The scene was set. Going through to the bathroom she took a long, refreshing shower. Slipping into a cerise kaftan she'd bought from Carmel's boutique, she felt cool, and added a black and silver necklace and silver sandals. After brushing her long hair and adding a spray of perfume, she was ready. Back in the kitchen, she turned on the oven to heat in preparation for the lamb.

In the distance she heard a low rumble of thunder and was aware of a brief flash of lightning. Then the rains began.

Looking out to the front, she saw that wraiths of steam rose from the now-emptying Bay Street. She watched as two young cyclists pedalled furiously then, lifting their legs, they skimmed through the warm rain as it hit the surface of the road, spraying fountains of water into the air from under the spinning wheels. Laura smiled. Now the rain fell with an intensity she had never experienced, crashing down on the corrugated roof of Orient View with a deafening roar and dripping down the windows. Looking out to the back, the usual calm waters of the Caribbean Sea now looked menacing as the lightning flared across the bay from a deep purple sky.

A set of headlights lit up the courtyard as a car pulled in, a door opened and closed again, and the car drove off. The next minute Blake appeared in the doorway, his hair and face soaked and large blotches of rain on his indigo shirt. He was carrying a bottle of wine in each hand. As he lowered his head to kiss her, a waft of heavenly scent hit her nose. They both laughed in surprise as an almighty thunderclap shook the windows and caused the light to flicker. Laura hoped the storm wasn't an omen for the evening ahead.

Following her to the kitchen, Blake put the wine on the worktop.

"I've brought Argentinian Malbec." He began to open a bottle to allow it to breathe.

"I hope you've brought a good appetite."

"I have," he said, "and something smells good."

Laura handed him a towel for his hair, and a hairdryer for his shirt.

"Some storm. Are you okay, Laura?" he asked above the din of the dryer.

"I love it." She realised instantly that Blake had probably come by early to check on her, and in truth she was glad he was there. Bringing the wine to the table, he poured two glasses. He handed one to Laura and their fingers brushed when he gave her the glass, sending a tingling reaction through her.

"Here's to a good night," he said, taking a sip of wine. He seemed in good spirits. *Tonight is not going to be easy,* Laura thought. Blake sat down on a dining chair, putting his elbows on the arms and placing his hands together, his fingers touching gently.

"You know, Laura, usually when I want to eat in, I have to get a meal delivered, so this is a real treat for me."

"I hope you can say that after you've tasted it," she quipped.

Laura guessed Blake was being polite, so she resisted the urge to suggest he could always cook something for himself. She reckoned there were many young women who would give their eye teeth to spend an evening with Blake, let alone to have the chance to cook for him. She'd seen the way they looked at him, wanting him to notice them. How when he spoke to them their eyes sparkled, and their smiles became wide and coy. Blake certainly had sex appeal in spades. Yet here she was on tenterhooks at the prospect of the evening ahead.

For around half an hour it seemed the storm was directly overhead. As it slowly moved away, the noise became fainter and the dramatic deluge ceased, leaving the air cooler and fresher. It was the perfect end to a sweltering day and her first tropical storm. It had been magnificent! And shared with Blake. She opened the veranda door and the air was filled with the sweet smells of magnolia and jasmine.

Bringing through the grilled oysters, Laura watched Blake carefully as he tried one. "Real good, never had cooked oysters before."

So the meal got off to a good start, the wine flowed, and all was going well. Laura began to feel calmer.

"Time for singing hinnies."

"For what?"

"Singing hinnies," repeated Laura, enjoying the joke. "Hinnie means honey, or pet, a term of endearment."

"What do they do, dare I ask?"

"They sing."

"Of course they do."

Laura popped two hinnies in a pan of butter. As the fat in the scone mixture heated, the bubbles began to whistle.

"What the heck?" exclaimed Blake.

As the warbling from the pan continued, Laura added two more and the discordant whistle became more of a passionate shriek. Blake's shoulders began to shake as he tried to suppress his laughter.

"They're having a good time," he managed to say. "I've never heard anything like it in my life – well, not from a scone."

His comment made her giggle as she brought the now-silent hinnies to the table with fresh cream.

"It seems cruel to eat them, they've entertained us so well," he mused.

Laura wondered how the rest of the evening would turn out. They moved to the comfortable seating. Blake seemed especially happy and at ease, and Laura told him so.

"You're easy to be with, Laura, I can forget life's pressures for a while."

"What is it you find so stressful?"

"Several things, usually family. I think you've gathered that by now." His demeanour changed slightly; his jaw tensed.

"I have," she replied. "Although you haven't exactly told me the reason why." Whatever there was between Blake and his family, it was not good. Laura wanted to know.

"It's complicated." Blake was trying to fob her off.

"Try me," she challenged.

"Okay," he began slowly. "As you know, my great-grandfather in Seattle started the family fortune in real estate. When he died, my grandfather took over. He moved the family to New York and when he died my father inherited. Like his father before him, my dad is a ruthless entrepreneur and has built a property empire. When I left Harvard I was expected to join."

"Understandable," said Laura. "So, what's the problem?"

"The problem is I don't want to be owned by my family, or to live and work in my father's shadow."

"Makes sense," she said.

"Not to my parents. Wealthy people like control, Laura. After Harvard, I joined the US Air Force and never went back home. My parents were appalled, but there was nothing they could do. They feel I rebelled against everything that was expected of me and ever since there has been friction between us."

"Growing up with my grandma, I didn't have that problem. There was no family business."

"Different worlds," he said. Blake paused briefly; he was usually more circumspect, he had never opened up about family in this way before. Then again, he had never met anyone like Laura.

"There's more," he sighed. "There are certain rules to live by in 'high society'. Philanthropy, for instance, is a way of life. Charity balls, galas, events usually organised by the women, all very commendable, but they in fact become a focus for their social life." Blake paused momentarily to look at Laura, uncertainty in his eyes.

Laura sighed; their backgrounds could not be further apart.

"Connections are therefore vital. It can be a very superficial society. My mother's concern for social status is all-consuming. All of which means that who you marry becomes so important. My mother hasn't forgiven me or given up on me. She would marry me off to someone she considers 'suitable' in a New York heartbeat."

"Perhaps," said Laura soothingly, "your parents just want what is best for you."

"Or best for them," Blake retorted, eyes glinting.

"That's harsh, Blake."

"I like to make my own decisions and choices in life. I see how they've almost ruined my sister's life. I love my parents, Laura, I do, but there is a darker side to family. You can struggle to find your own identity, especially in families like mine. I don't fit in. I try to keep them at arm's length."

"That doesn't sound healthy, Blake."

"It works for me." He was defiant.

Blake had opened up to Laura and she felt a bond had started to develop between them that she didn't want to lose. She was taken aback at the mention of a sister but didn't want to pry further. However, it seemed inconceivable to her that Blake could harbour such animosity towards his parents. She felt saddened.

"One thing I realise more than I ever wanted to is that family is important."

"I think that ship has sailed," he said.

"After my grandmother died, I have never felt so alone," she said softly.

Laura's gentle admonishment echoed in Blake's ears and he recognised he must have come across as insensitive. Although he remained silent, Laura knew her words had touched him.

"I'm sorry," he said, looking slightly abashed. "Didn't you say you have something you want to discuss with me?" Blake's dark eyes watched her. He sensed her vulnerability. He had no idea what was coming.

As a rule, Laura did not like to prevaricate but she hesitated, wondering if tonight was a good time to say what she had in mind. Her throat went dry and she felt a wave of anxiety but, she reasoned, it was time for some honesty here.

"You know, Blake," she began, clearing her throat, "you were the first person I met when I arrived in Barbados."

Blake flinched a little – he wondered where this was heading.

Laura reached for her wine, hoping Blake hadn't noticed that her hand was shaking.

"I don't want to sound presumptuous; I apologise if I do. I just want to try to convey my state of mind to you." *Clumsy,* she thought. Looking squarely at him, Laura swallowed. She searched for the right words but, as was usual when talking about her feelings, she failed to find them. Instead she heard herself blurting, "I don't want to mislead you. I need to make it clear I'm not looking to get involved with anyone."

She hadn't meant to be so direct. Knowing she hadn't explained herself very well at all, she tried to make sense of her thoughts.

"What I'm really trying to say, Blake, is that your friendship is important to me."

Her blue eyes cast an embarrassed look. She waited with bated breath. Blake remained unruffled.

"Good to know," he said, a hint of amusement in his voice. He hoped Laura hadn't caught the flash of guilt in his eyes. From the moment they first met Laura had spurred a gut-level response in him. For Blake, this was not what he expected to hear and he was fazed for a moment. He ran his fingers through his hair and struggled to think it through, but his mind went blank. He couldn't remember the last time he had been faced with a woman who perhaps was prepared to refuse him. What was it about Laura? She had got inside his head and he didn't know how this would play out.

"I got it. I understand." Or he thought he did. Blake knew his women, though he never let anyone get close. But this was a first. He was more used to young women clamouring for his attention. Laura was offering friendship, which intrigued him. He smiled ruefully – it was a route he had never taken, never needed to, never wanted to. It would be new to him. Yet he was willing to accept. This lovely young woman from a tiny island he had never heard of had managed to sideline him. The frustration he felt did nothing to dampen his desire; if anything it made him want her more. Next week, he hoped they would be in Trinidad together. *Who knows?* he thought. *Further down the line…*

Laura hadn't been prepared for the conversation with Blake to leave her feeling so tense. She may have established the boundaries for their friendship but she realised she was falling into the trap again of overthinking everything. *Why can't I just go with the flow – just feel?*

It was late, and Blake decided he'd better call it a night before he gave in to the urge to pull Laura into his arms. Just after midnight, his cab drew up outside.

"Are we good, Laura?" he asked.

"Yes, of course we are," Laura replied.

Friends, she'd said. Blake smiled. "So, my friend," he teased, "would you still like to come to Trinidad?"

"I'd love to if you still want to take me?"

"You bet!" he replied.

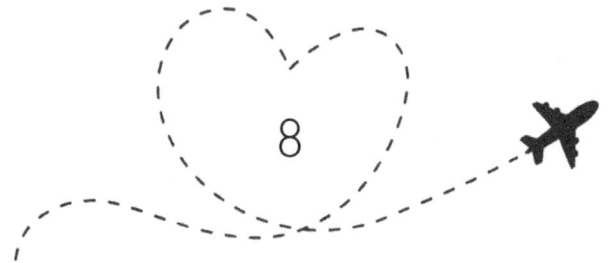

8

At St. Catherine's, Emma and Laura were reaching the end of a meeting with Erika. They had been invited to her office to discuss the possibility of extending the inventory for the school library.

"We are so lucky at St. Catherine's," Erika said. "We have a library well stocked with course books for the senior school, as well as classroom shelves full of readers for the lower school reading schemes."

"I understand," said Laura. "If only it were possible to include more fiction, poetry books, and books on a wider variety of topics."

"Even the best of schools rarely have sufficient budget to buy the books they would like, especially as pupil numbers grow," Erika sighed.

"We need to extend," Emma interjected. "If a child's parents cannot afford to buy books and the school library is limited, plus they don't have the opportunity to visit a public library, how can a child read for pleasure?"

"True," Erika sighed again. "We have always placed great emphasis on developing reading skills. But all schools are battling cuts."

"We're very much about the physical book," Laura wanted Erika to know. "The book I lent Dulcie was given to me by my grandmother, there's history to it."

"I agree," said Emma. "There's something special about reading a well-thumbed book, knowing that so many before you have read and enjoyed it. You feel a connection."

"I know, I know," laughed Erika. "I'm with you both. And in our throwaway society that is a very good point. Your arguments are sound. Leave it with me. I will bring the matter up at the next governors' meeting."

Laura and Emma had been relentless but felt the discussion had been fruitful and that they had conveyed their concerns clearly. Now it was up to the governors.

"It's time we weren't here," said Emma, heading towards the main entrance of the school. "How about we catch up tonight? I'll bring a bottle, we can celebrate something," she laughed.

"Sounds like a plan," replied Laura.

"I'll come about seven. You can tell me what's between you and Blake."

Laura exhaled and pursed her lips. "We're friends. That's it."

– – –

That evening, Emma climbed the steps to Laura's veranda waving a bottle of red wine ceremoniously in her hand.

"No need to ask you how life's treating you," said Laura. "You're positively glowing, turquoise suits you." She was trying to distract Emma with a charm offensive.

"All Ivan's doing and one of Carmel's kaftans."

"There's a gleam in your eyes," laughed Laura.

Opening the bottle and pouring, Laura handed Emma a glass of wine and then poured one for herself.

"That gleam is probably curiosity. Come on, spill, Laura, what's going on with you and Blake?"

Laura sighed. So much for the charm offensive. "Nothing's going on."

"It doesn't look like nothing, he calls round all the time. He can't seem to keep away," laughed Emma.

"He could lose interest just as quickly," sighed Laura. "I don't want to risk getting hurt, I feel safe just as friends."

"Really, Laura? Come on. No one offers to fly you to Trinidad in a private jet unless they want to sleep with you," Emma smiled cheekily.

"Blake is just being nice," said Laura.

"Of course, but it doesn't change the fact," replied Emma.

"That's as may be, but in my experience men and women can be good friends. Otherwise, it would be ridiculous; half the world's population would be lost to the friendship pool. Besides, Emma, a trip to Trini Carnival is a trip to Trini Carnival. When will I get another chance like this? I really want to go – with my friend Blake," she said pointedly.

"Hang on," said Emma. "Have you thought this through?"

"Yes, I have," replied Laura. "And I've spoken at length to Blake. He knows the score. Not everything in life is about the bedroom."

"Dream on," retorted Emma.

Laura took a gulp of her wine. She was feeling a little uncomfortable talking about Blake in this way.

"Fair enough," Emma conceded. "Enjoy Trinidad." Emma raised her glass. "With your friend Blake," she added as an aside.

Laura screwed up her nose, smiled and changed the subject.

"What about you and Ivan?" she asked.

"We're good, but who knows what's coming round the corner."

"Well, tomorrow it's probably a large van," said Laura. "Remember we're helping Sean to move."

"Oh yeah," said Emma.

– – –

Next morning they were waiting patiently on the patio, when at last they heard a vehicle rattle to a stop in the courtyard and the figures of Sean and Ivan appeared. Sean called out to them as he approached.

"Ready for my big day, girls?"

He was clearly in high spirits, much to Laura's relief. He'd confided that living on top of work in the hospital digs had become difficult for him – he felt claustrophobic, he knew he had to get out. Luckily, he had managed to find a small house in a nice little area of Rockley. Being further back from the beach meant the rent was quite reasonable. A new milestone in his life. Sean had never had his own place before. It seemed that everyone had become involved in his change of residence, including Laura and Emma.

Ensconced in the front seat of the van, their first port of call was to Carmel's boutique. She was updating the décor at the Yellow Bird and a perfectly good yellow sofa was going spare, along with matching curtains from the fitting rooms, which Sean was delighted to accept. A quick coffee and chat with Carmel and they loaded the items. Sean turned the van and headed towards Paradise Heights, where Marvin met them with a cheery smile and a couple of saucepans. Marvin and Carmel had gone through their effects room by room, identifying anything that could be passed on to Sean. This turned out to be two pink floral rattan chairs no one used anymore, a pink rug, two old dining chairs and, of course, the pans. Sean took the lot. A cool drink and exchange of pleasantries with Marvin and they loaded the van and set off towards the hospital.

Sean's room was on the second floor of the two-storeyed residence block in the hospital grounds. He stopped outside a half-open door, pushing it open as far as it would go, and they squeezed in. Laura's eyes opened wide as she was met by a sea of clutter. There were boxes everywhere, and here and there a suitcase. The room was small; a single bed along one side was piled high with clothes. There was a tiny wardrobe, two chairs and a table in the centre of the room, and a bookcase. A pair of sliding glass doors opened onto a narrow balcony with an airing rack for laundry.

"My wardrobe is bigger than this room, Sean," she said, looking around in astonishment.

"Yeah, not much room in the dorms, it's only temporary accommodation," said Ivan, pushing a box out of the way with his foot.

"No room for a person, that's for sure, and what's that smell?" asked Emma, crinkling her nose.

"Disinfectant," replied Sean flatly. "A real passion killer! Lately I've become acutely more conscious of things I never paid much attention to before. Everything about this room is getting to me. I'm more than ready to leave."

Keen to get started, Sean lifted two suitcases. Following his lead, they soon made short work of collecting his things. As the last bin bag of clothing was thrown into the back of the van, Sean turned to his friends, grinning like a Cheshire Cat.

"I cannot believe I'm out of here," he said.

As they drove away, Laura noticed that he didn't look back.

The four of them were crammed onto the long front seat of the now-heavily-laden van. It rocked to and fro under Sean's erratic driving as he bumped his way through the traffic. Suddenly, without warning, he swerved quickly to the left and into a quiet lane.

"Oops, nearly missed the turn," he chuckled.

Laura closed her eyes and held Emma's hand.

"Careful, Sean," said Ivan firmly. "We don't want to end up in a ditch where no one finds us for days."

"That won't happen," he quipped. "We're not on an Irish stag do."

Finally, and not a moment too soon for the others, Sean pulled up with a skid and a screech onto a driveway. The late morning sun cast a golden glow over a modest whitewashed villa and the grassed area around. Laura thought the effect was very beautiful.

"Welcome to my new abode," Sean said proudly.

Laura and Emma scrambled out like a pair of scolded cats, keen to explore but more relieved to be on terra firma again.

"Never again," mumbled Ivan under his breath.

The sweet smell of frangipani greeted Laura's nostrils as she walked towards the porch. In the slightly unkempt front garden she was aware of a hummingbird fluttering in the hibiscus, as though in welcome. She had the distinct feeling that this little house had been waiting for someone to come and look after it.

The solid mahogany front door was situated inside a porch. In keeping with this older style, it opened immediately onto the kitchen, in which there was a fridge and a cooker, a table and four chairs. Along one wall there was a shelf, with hooks underneath for hanging pans. An archway led to a dimly lit living room.

"It's a bit musty, it's been empty for a while," said Sean, drawing apart the wooden shutter to open a window. Instantly the sun streamed in, flooding the room with light. Sean flicked a switch and, with a faint whirring noise, the ceiling fan began to move slowly as if roused from a deep sleep.

"Hey, not bad at all," said Ivan, now able to see the room clearly.

"It's a good size."

"It is that," agreed Sean.

"Can we look around, Sean?" Emma asked.

"Be my guests, I'll start unloading."

A corridor led to a small, white-tiled, clean bathroom and two bedrooms, one of which was painted green. Each contained a double bed and a mahogany wardrobe. The furniture, once expensive, now looked old yet dignified.

"How much to bet Sean goes for the green bedroom," laughed Emma.

"I love this house, it's so quirky," said Laura.

"It's so Sean," agreed Emma.

The bedroom windows overlooked a small garden at the back. A huge pink bougainvillea draped itself over a wire fence, metres away from a glorious display of flowers in the garden next door.

Returning to join the others, Laura and Emma helped to empty the van and arrange the furniture. Clothes were put in the wardrobes, linen in the bedrooms, towels in the bathroom. The two pink rattan chairs and rug adorned the living room, whilst the yellow sofa literally stole the limelight. Glancing around, Laura smiled to herself; everything was a complete mismatch. The room looked – well – strange, yet comfortable at the same time, even cosy.

Ivan sat down on the sofa.

"You seem to attract a lot of yellow, Sean," he said drily.

Sean could not have cared less. He stood back and marvelled.

"It looks grand, doesn't it?"

"Only if you're colour-blind or on hallucinatory drugs," joked Ivan.

Sean grinned. Laura glanced at him and caught an expression of pure joy in his eyes.

"I think this room looks as cheerful as the new occupant," she said, giving Sean a hug.

"That sums it up perfectly," he said. "Come on, let's celebrate."

Sean insisted they stay and eat – he had bought "stuff" in especially, he told them. He wouldn't take no for an answer.

"You cook as well?" Laura asked, surprised. "You have hidden depths, Sean."

"I do, I'm a good catch, Laura." He winked at her.

Laura felt a rush of affection for Sean. Simple as it was, he was so thrilled with his new home. He was such a genuine, kind person. She felt lucky to have him in her life.

Crowded in among the empty packing boxes, Laura, Ivan and Emma sat in the psychedelic living room and watched as Sean drummed up a meal of fried fish and vegetables for them.

"I feel this house loves having people," he called over the sizzle of the frying pan.

"This house has been waiting for you," Emma called back to him.

They ate and drank, polishing off two bottles of red wine in the process. Ivan called a toast.

"Here's to your new home, Sean, may you be very happy here!"

"Thank you, guys, for your help today," he said, raising his glass. The old Sean was back.

Back at Orient View, Laura opened the veranda doors and surveyed the scene with smiling eyes. What a day! Fun, laughter, friends – she wanted that. And next week, Trinidad Carnival. It seemed to Laura that life could hardly be better.

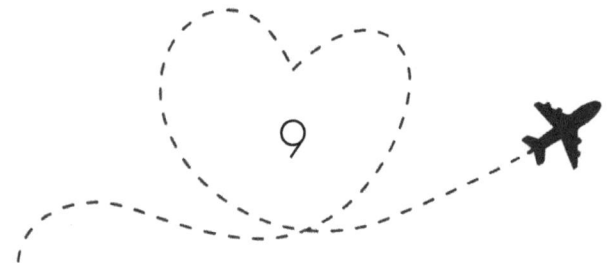

Climbing the stairway to the private jet, Laura was welcomed aboard by a smiling steward, who introduced himself as Tom. Turning to enter the cabin she found she had stepped into a world of opulence. It was a large, airy space with circular windows along each side, caramel carpet throughout and large cream leather seats with a mahogany table between them. Sitting down and surveying her surroundings from her comfortable armchair, Laura could see a small white, fitted kitchen visible through an archway. The sumptuous smell of new leather and subtle perfume heightened her excitement. The jet was luxurious. She felt a flutter in her stomach. As much as she loved it, she could not have felt more out of her comfort zone.

After storing their luggage and exchanging a quick word with Tom, Blake sat down opposite her. Laura looked across at him, and his eyes softened when they met hers. He gave her a steady gaze. Lowering her eyes, she was conscious of a pink flush rising in her cheeks.

Into the flight, Tom served a light meal of grilled chicken salad, cheese and crackers, fruit and coffee. It was all special for Laura, although she realised with more than a little discomfort that this was Blake's world, he was totally at ease. One hour later, on a balmy starlit night, they touched down in Port of Spain. Leaving the aircraft, Laura felt the warm Trinidadian air hit her face. The VIP treatment continued throughout Piarco Airport, and outside a chauffeur-driven car arrived for them. Was this business as usual for Blake? Or had he gone all out to impress her? She was certainly impressed.

"Your chariot awaits," he grinned. A short drive and they arrived at the Seaview Mansions Building, where an elevator took them directly to Blake's penthouse suite. The entire journey had been hassle-free.

Walking through the door of the penthouse, Laura swept her eyes admiringly over a bright and spacious room as Blake switched on the lights. Two elegant, white sofas were arranged around a large cream rug, a cubed coffee table in the centre. A black grand piano was placed next to a floor-to-ceiling window, which offered a spectacular panoramic view over the nearby coastline. The dining room, too, was luminescent. Laura watched as the colours of the rainbow refracted through the crystals of the chandelier and danced onto the walls. The table was beautifully set for eight people. A state-of-the-art kitchen lay beyond. Terraces with more seating and large plants offered private outside space. Laura was in awe of the luxurious appearance of Blake's penthouse.

"It's magnificent, Blake," she gushed.

"Glad you like it," he replied.

"Mind you," she added, "it doesn't look lived in."

"It isn't," Blake answered.

"What a waste," she shrugged.

She looked around at the gleaming chrome, the highly polished floors, the crystal-clear glass in the windows. It screamed "high maintenance" to Laura.

"Have you got an army of cleaners coming in daily?" she asked airily.

"No way. I like my privacy. The building management prepare everything before I arrive and send in a cleaner when I leave."

"Jammy," said Laura.

Blake laughed, not sure what she'd said.

"Have you always liked things this neat and tidy?"

"Hell no, at Harvard my place was full of empties, but five years in the Air Force helps you clean up your act."

"Good," she replied, referring to the empties. She had always been irritated by anyone who was overly neat and tidy.

Laura needn't have worried about sleeping arrangements either. The anxiety she had built up in her mind fell away as Blake showed her to her bedroom with en-suite. He seemed highly entertained as he saw the tension leave her face and she began to relax.

"When you've showered, there's robes and slippers in the closet."

"Of course there are." Laura shot him a cheeky look.

Blake laughed. "See you downstairs," he said.

Yes, Blake's penthouse was on two levels.

Blake had champagne waiting when she returned to the lounge. She was wearing her black, raw-silk trouser suit, which was light and cool, and not the robe and slippers Blake had boldly suggested. His eyes drifted over her. "You look beautiful," he said.

"Thank you," she replied.

"Find everything to your liking?" he asked.

"Sumptuous room, gorgeous bathroom, Egyptian cotton sheets. What's not to like?" Her eyes danced with amusement.

They went out onto the terrace to enjoy the warmth of the evening. Blake took the Dom Pérignon and two glasses with him. They sipped champagne watching the night glow of the buildings, bars and restaurants along by the sea. The mood was relaxed.

"You know, Blake, our worlds could not be more different," she said casually.

"But we're the same underneath, we're human," he joked.

"Perhaps the similarity ends there," Laura teased.

"Now you're killing me," he laughed. "But seriously, we both want to give meaning to our lives, don't we?"

"You're beginning to sound like an ordinary person, Blake."

"I am an ordinary person," he smiled. "That's why I need to do my own thing – the business, I mean."

"Does that make you happy?"

"What do you think happiness is, Laura? I'm interested," he replied.

"I'm not sure. I just know you can't switch it on. It sort

of creeps up on you when you least expect it. In literature they talk about 'grasping' or 'snatching' at happiness, as though it's some disembodied entity flying around. Something that isn't really ours to take."

"Heavy stuff," he laughed.

"Well, what do you think?" she asked him.

Blake took a sip of champagne before replying. "I'm more of a pleasure man myself. You know what you're getting and you enjoy it at the time," he chuckled.

"But isn't that a bit like having a drink, it's not long before you want another one?"

Laura smiled at him.

"Not quite, but sometimes," Blake said, lifting his glass to her. They both laughed together. Blake was enjoying talking to Laura. She had a quaint way of expressing herself that charmed him.

They continued chatting until eventually Laura grew tired and decided to call it a night.

"I enjoyed tonight, Blake, thank you for inviting me."

"I did too, here's to a good weekend."

They both stood up hesitantly, and the movement was slightly awkward. Blake looked at her and he felt a little nervous. He resisted the strong urge to sweep her into his arms and kiss her. He knew that if he did she would never trust him again. For the first time in his life, he didn't want that. Instead, he moved towards her; their eyes met for a second and he inhaled the fragrance of her perfume.

"It's been a long day," he said.

He gave her a chaste goodnight kiss on the cheek. Laura breathed a small sigh. True to his word, Blake had kept things on a friendly basis. As she turned to leave, she knew Blake's eyes were still on her and she felt a strange twitching in her stomach. Blake watched her go – the young woman who was turning his world upside down. He poured himself another drink and sat for a while. Laura was charming company and he realised how much he liked her. He began to regret the whimsical approach he had taken towards her. Leaning back, he downed the rest of his drink and headed to bed.

The next morning Laura awoke around ten, which was late for her. She quickly showered and cleaned her teeth. Pulling on a black, bare-shouldered top and white shorts, she put a brush through her hair and slipped into her sandals. Going downstairs, she found Blake in the kitchen sipping coffee with Charlie and Monica, who greeted her warmly with a hug. She caught Blake giving her an appreciative look and she immediately felt self-conscious.

"Good afternoon," he teased. "I guess you slept well. There's fresh coffee," he said, pouring her a cup.

"Really well, thanks, that bed is so comfortable."

"These guys have planned our day," Blake laughed, nodding towards Charlie and Monica.

"Well, we thought we'd head to the Waterfront for a 'Trini lunch' first," Monica told her. "We can easily walk from here. Later, we would like to show you the bird sanctuary."

"You okay with that, Laura?" Blake asked.

"Sounds lovely," she replied.

"Give me a minute," Laura said, turning to leave, "I've forgotten something."

She emerged moments later wearing her red straw hat.

"Great hat," he said, tweaking a strand of hair from under the brim.

Laura wrinkled her nose and laughed, "You'll never lose me in a crowd."

"Is that right?" Blake said wryly, pretending to duck under the large brim as she turned around.

As they left the Seaview Mansions building, Monica walked with Laura, linking her arm whilst Blake and Charlie were ahead, discussing the approaching financial year end for the business.

"You and Blake must be getting on well, Laura. He's never brought a girl to the penthouse before."

"Yes, we've become friends," Laura replied.

"You don't mean just friends, though, do you?" Monica cajoled.

"I do," said Laura. *Not this again*, she thought.

"Just friends!" exclaimed Monica. "Is that possible?"

"I don't see why not," said Laura.

"Are you joking? Are we talking about the same Blake?" said Monica in disbelief, stopping in her tracks and letting go of Laura's arm.

"But why?" Laura felt this was neither the appropriate time nor place to start explaining the way she felt and hoped Monica would leave it at that.

"But how can you resist him?" They both laughed but Laura didn't reply. "Sorry, it's not my business," said Monica, sensing her friend's reticence.

Tucking her arm through Laura's, Monica hurried them along to catch up with the others.

"Just friends," she muttered under her breath. "I bet that's a first for Blake."

They walked leisurely for about ten minutes through the back streets, arriving at a cosy local restaurant on a promenade overlooking the sea. A table had been reserved for them. Laura loved the décor. Stone-flagged floor, large palm plants surrounding tables set with blue and white china plates and silver candlesticks. Sideboards filled with glasses and decanters. It felt more like being in someone's home rather than a restaurant. Monica was animated as they sat down at their table.

"Trini food is a fusion of all our cultures, such as African, Creole, Syrian and Italian – my family came from Greece. We are so diverse," she explained.

Much like the décor, thought Laura. Charlie ordered mineral water for them all. Laura had noticed that Charlie and Blake didn't drink much alcohol and Blake certainly none during the day.

Before too long a waiter arrived with a large oval dish covered with chunks of "geera pork" seasoned with cumin seeds, peppers, onions and chives. Another put down a large plate of chilli lime chicken. Glass bowls of rice and salads followed, the lettuce seasoned with sapodilla fruit, giving it a lovely malty smell. This was the set lunch menu. Now the table was full and they began to eat. The other customers all seemed to know each other and a friendly buzz of conversation accompanied the food. They ate and drank and ordered more water to combat the chilli. It was a wonderful lunch and intro to Trini food for Laura. They talked and laughed; Laura loved it, she needed that, she felt at ease. She told Monica how much she had enjoyed it.

"We haven't finished yet," said Monica, surprised. "There's more."

The second course was delayed to give them a short rest. After a while, a large plate of Kurmas – a small, crispy, sweet doughnut – was put down in front of them alongside pone cassava, a mixture of cassava root, coconut, sugar, spices and raisins. The lunch continued. Laura noticed Monica glancing around the table from time to time to make sure they were enjoying themselves. Blake too would catch her eyes and smile. Laura watched as Charlie left his seat and stooped to whisper something in Monica's ear and saw her swiftly look up at him and smile. Laura's heart warmed to see how deeply smitten they were with each other. Charlie discreetly slipped away to settle the bill. It seemed to Laura that her "Trini chow" education was complete. A quick peek at the time and she realised they had been in the restaurant for nearly three hours.

The chauffeur-driven car arrived outside and, leaving Port of Spain, they took a leisurely drive south-west of the town and into countryside before arriving at the nature reserve. Leaving the car, they walked a short distance to where a wooden boat and a local guide was waiting for them.

As she stepped into the boat, the pungent smell of rotten eggs filled Laura's nostrils and made her eyes water.

"Hydrogen sulphide from rotting vegetation," Blake explained.

Now far from the frantic pace of Trinidad's capital,

Laura found she was entering a mystical world of nature as they began their journey along the miles of waterways. Laura turned and looked towards the swamps. Huge trees lined the water's edge, their spreading boughs covering prolific undergrowth beneath as mangroves melded and matted with mud. The dark shadows made her shiver with fear, it looked dank and mysterious as if never penetrated by man. Laura stared into the tangle of trunks and leaves – there was movement, but she was not sure what it was until one of the trunks seemed to unwind itself and slide through the undergrowth. It was a snake, a boa crawling through the vines. She shuddered; there was something primeval about these marshlands. Pink flamingos, herons and egrets pecked for food at the water's edge, a hawk eagle sat regally on a branch. Occasionally they would hear a rustle of feathers as parrots flew between trees. A crocodile-like creature showed its head above water, making Laura breathe sharply in fright. "A caimen," the guide told them. Blake put his arm around her in a reassuring gesture. Only the sound of the boat's engine broke the quiet spell that had fallen over them.

Moving deep into the centre of the swamp, they entered a large lake. Turning off the engine, their guide explained that they would wait here for the scarlet ibis, the national bird of Trinidad. The bright red colour, he told them, comes from the crustaceans they eat.

"Each day," he said, "these magnificent birds fly eleven miles to Venezuela to feed and return late afternoon to the mangrove swamps to roost."

They didn't have to wait long; within minutes the

sky began to fill with scarlet feathers as hundreds of ibis flew above their heads against the backdrop of a red and golden sunset, their strange cries echoing around the lake. Landing in the trees, they gave the appearance of brilliant red flowers hanging among the foliage. The sheer beauty of nature around her was a very emotional experience for Laura and her eyes filled with tears. Blake took her hand and squeezed it gently.

"Watch out for your hat," he joked.

Laura knew she would never forget this beautiful and unique experience, not only because of the scarlet ibis, still flying home over the lake, but because of the friends she had shared it with.

The next day was Monday and the first day of the carnival in Trinidad. Under Monica's guidance they threaded their way through the busy streets of Port of Spain, passing local stores, Rastafarian fruit traders in their vivid outfits, kiosks selling drinks. The warm breeze carried the aroma of chicken curry rotis and Kachoris, cooked on hot plates by the roadside. Eventually they arrived at the main route for the carnival. Already a mass of large trucks carrying steel bands, calypso bands and DJs blasting their music from the back were winding slowly along. Youngsters pushing carts with oil drums on them followed the trucks, and behind them all, crowds of dancers were doing "jump up". Finding it impossible to be a spectator for long, Monica persuaded them to join the throng. The narrow roads were bursting with the music and sounds of merrymakers. After an hour or so of "jump up" Monica led them to a street café to sit down.

"See Trini Carnival and die," she said dramatically, flopping into her seat.

A short rest and she was up again and pulling Charlie with her. They all paused for a second before braving the streets once more.

The highlight of the carnival was the parade. They stood by the side of the road as a multitude of the most extraordinary costumes passed them. Purples, oranges, reds, fluorescent greens: a kaleidoscope of colours. Some dancers wore huge headdresses, some more than two metres wide. Laura had never seen anything like it in her life, she didn't know how they managed to hold their heads up. Revellers streamed up and down the roads. They could hardly move in the throng and Laura could feel the crowd closing in on them. Blake took her arm.

"No need to go to Rio," Monica called to them above the din. "It's all here in Trini," she said proudly. *Indeed it is,* reflected Laura, her senses now overloaded and her body heavy with fatigue, but her heart was filled with joy.

Late Tuesday afternoon Blake and Laura said goodbye to Charlie and Monica and took a taxi to Piarco Airport. Where the jet was waiting for their return trip to Barbados. They were both exhausted. The last few days had been tumultuous and wonderful for Laura. The music, the dancing, the vibrancy of the carnival had been one surreal moment after another. She had dipped her toe into Blake's world and it was so different from anything she knew. It made her feel that, until now, she had been watching life from the sidelines.

Now seated on the plane, Blake seemed quiet and

pensive. He wondered – had he shown too much of himself to Laura? Was it a mistake to bring her here?

"You okay, Laura?" he asked.

"Yes, why?" she replied.

"You have a faraway look in your eyes."

"Sorry," she said absently.

As she watched the play of light from the setting sun on Blake's face, Laura thought how charismatic he could be. How much she had enjoyed his company. The plane took off and Trinidad disappeared through the clouds. Leaning back in her seat, she drifted into sleep.

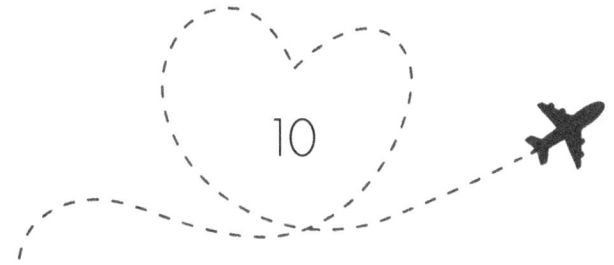

10

Blake looked down from his parents' penthouse at the cherry blossom trees now in full bloom in Central Park. An explosion of delicate pink flowers covered the branches, petals spreading like snowflakes on the grass beneath. He marvelled how the transient beauty of nature could transform an everyday scene into something magical. Blake had spent two days in New York visiting his parents, and as much as he loved this exciting city, that was more than enough.

His parents, William and Rhonda Degas, belonged to the wealthy elite. His father had built up a property empire, which Blake had resolutely refused to be part of, although Blake had agreed to fly a shipment of goods for him into Barbados. The favour was a manipulation of sorts by William, to try to coax Blake into joining the family business or merging their two companies. William Degas was a man used to getting his own way.

On the other hand, his mother, Rhonda, had her own

agenda: to marry him off, but not just to anyone – oh no! To a young woman of her choosing. Blake had received several invitations to dinner on his fleeting visit, from family friends keen to introduce their daughters. Blake declined them all. Not to be out-manoeuvred, his mother arranged for one of these young women to drop by the penthouse later.

"Serena is going to call in after tennis at the club," Rhonda told him airily. Blake felt slightly irritated. "I'm not telling you to marry her, just give her another chance. She really likes you," Rhonda urged. Blake's emphatic "no" was just ignored as she continued, "Be nice to Serena, her mother is my friend. You could do a lot worse; Serena understands our world."

Blake knew exactly what his mother meant: *her family is wealthy*. He had grown up with the cautions of his mother ringing in his ears, "Beware of social climbers, gold diggers!" He had learnt to accept her paranoia, but it had left him unsure whether women were in fact more interested in his wealth than in him. The doubts planted by his mother had now become second nature to him. Blake had learned long ago to submerge his emotions when it came to the women in his life.

Arriving early and certainly not from tennis, Serena was dressed to impress. She was wearing long black boots and a slinky, ruby-coloured dress, which flattered her slender figure and complimented her long blonde hair and pale blue eyes that, with a mere flutter, could entice. She looked sensational. Blake was vaguely aware of the outline of her breasts and nipples through the tight fabric; Serena had curves and she knew how to use them. She flashed Blake a full-on smile, a hardly disguised come-on, yet Blake's mind was pre-occupied with thoughts of his time in Trinidad with Laura, who seemed out of reach. This was going to be a long afternoon; Serena was on a mission.

"That was such a good weekend we had, Blake. I love Barbados."

"Good to hear." He did his best to sound indifferent.

"I'd love to get away again from this cold weather, cheer myself up," Serena sighed, addressing no one in particular. Blake was not prepared to take the bait, but his mother was.

"Why not invite Serena again? She'll be good company for you." There was very little that was subtle about Rhonda Degas.

Blake felt himself tense. His shoulders became rigid, but neither woman seemed to notice.

"I'm busy with work, I don't have much free time." He looked coolly at his mother and then at Serena.

"That's okay, I can go shopping, buy some exotic sarongs and swimwear. We're going to Nantucket for summer."

Blake remembered only too well Serena's shopping trips. A busy day for her was buying a new dress.

"How about I just come down now and again, when I can. I won't interfere with work, I promise," she pouted. Serena only wanted an open invite.

"What a good idea, you'll both have fun," Rhonda said artfully.

Blake's heart sank. He felt cornered, and to avoid

argument he agreed, curbing the urge to say what he really thought. The rest of the afternoon was dull for Blake. Thankfully Serena's driver arrived early to take her home. Mission accomplished, she left happy.

So Serena would come to Barbados whenever she wanted. How had she managed to pull that off? Only for a few days at a time, Blake hoped. Thankfully, the beach house was big. What harm could it do? Blake tried hard to look on the bright side.

Mid-morning the next day Blake climbed the steps to a large office block in Midtown Manhattan, where he had arranged to meet up with his father. Taking the elevator to the sixth floor, he opened a door and greeted the secretary. She gave him a charming smile and nodded towards a door.

"He's inside," she mouthed.

The office was spacious. On the walls were photographs and artist impressions of New York developments, some complete and others in various stages of development. To one side there was a large bookcase filled with heavy-looking books. Behind a huge oak desk filled with piles of paper and memos highlighted in yellow was the man himself, Bill Degas. Good-looking, tanned and silver-haired, he was wearing a light suit, with a gold Rolex watch visible on his left wrist. He was on the phone. He gestured for Blake to take a seat.

"How high is the development? How high do you want it?" he retorted in his usual gruff voice. Blake waited. Moments later he wrapped up the call and actually smiled at Blake.

"Sorry to interrupt," said Blake.

"No problem. All set for the flight tomorrow?" Bill asked.

"Sure, I fly early morning."

"Good, good," Bill replied, rubbing his eyes as if he hadn't slept in days. He picked up a brochure and tossed it to the front of the desk as if Blake was supposed to read it.

"New development. River North, mixed on two sites. Commercial, residential and retail, it's a truly spectacular project."

"I'm sure it is," said Blake. He knew what was coming next.

"We'll go take a look. It might excite you," said Bill. "Convince you to join us."

Blake doubted that. He knew he couldn't spend his days in an office poring over site plans surrounded by the massive concrete and glass structures of the cityscape.

"It's exciting – challenging," his father persisted.

"It's not for me." Blake stood his ground.

They had never been easy in each other's company. Blake felt that potential conflict always lay just beneath the surface.

"The skyline of New York is changing so rapidly. I see that as I fly in," said Blake.

"Progress, Blake, progress. In my world that's good news." He tapped his knuckles on the desk. Then, getting up, he walked to the window and gazed out. He paced along one wall of his office. He was his usual restless self.

"In fact, let's head down there now," he said.

"Fancy a coffee first? Ease up for a while," suggested Blake.

Bill flashed his eyes at him.

"I'll never ease up – I'm driven," he said with a chuckle. "Why would I? What else would I do? We'll grab a coffee later."

Blake shuddered at the thought – no time for coffee, what else would he do? His father's attitudes and opinions were so ingrained.

Bill informed his secretary that he was leaving. She nodded but asked no questions. No one asked Bill Degas why he did anything. They took the elevator down to the parking area where a driver was waiting. Blake shook his head in frustration as they drove away.

They headed north along the Henry Hudson Parkway for a few miles, and the driver then took the second exit before turning left onto a huge real estate project site. Collecting a hard hat and high-vis fluorescent vest from the office, Blake and his father walked among the noise, chaos and dust. Blake glanced up at the uncompleted bulk of a structural steel frame towering up fifty storeys or more in front of him. Bill was animated as they walked the concrete floors of the lower levels. He pointed out areas designated for residential, retail and commercial enterprises.

"We're building the future, Blake," he said proudly.

"It's certainly impressive," replied Blake.

"You could be part of it," suggested Bill.

"Development is not for me, Dad."

"It's a vast empire. Eventually you could take over, with my help," Bill continued.

Blake did not want his father's help. By the time he'd left Harvard, he didn't want anything from him.

"This whole lifestyle is just not me," he said calmly.

"Three generations of empire-building and you don't want to be part of it! How do you want to live?" Bill persisted.

"I want my life to be about my decisions – my choices. I have a life and a business which suits me just fine." Blake felt compelled to remind his father.

Bill shrugged. He was one of those people who didn't really listen.

"My father expected me to join the company and I did so, out of respect for him," said Bill irritably.

"Not so fast, Dad," said Blake. "I do respect you; I have a good deal of respect for you and what you've achieved. It's just not for me."

"That's disappointing," said Bill.

Blake inhaled deeply. It struck him that one thing he would like from his father was his approval, but he doubted he would ever get that.

Blake left his father conferring with the contractors. There was one more thing he wanted to do here in New York. He called a cab and gave his sister's address in East Hampton. He was nervous to see Kristina, but felt he couldn't put it off any longer.

– – –

The flight back to Barbados the next morning was uneventful for Blake. Leaving the confines of the cockpit he headed off to his car. He drove to his beach house, relieved finally to be back home in Barbados.

Wasting no time, he quickly changed into casual clothes and drove to his favourite diving spot. *The Berwyn*, a French tug, had sunk in Carlisle Bay in 1919 and the wreck had become an integral part of the ecosystem of the island, as it formed an artificial reef. Ironically, thought Blake, from a shipwreck now came riches for the Caribbean Sea. He found it to be so beautiful down there, swimming between the hard and soft coral. He was surrounded by vibrantly coloured tropical fish, sea horses, and both green and hawksbill turtles. Their colours and movement through and between the coral reef created a constantly changing underwater vista. For Blake it was the perfect way to unwind after New York.

– – –

Erika sat in her office enjoying the cooling benefit of the air from the revolving blades of the free-standing fan. Looking out of the window at the lush grounds of St. Catherine's, she felt a glow of satisfaction. She thought of the possibilities for the children that a new library would bring. Another chapter in the life of the school, a very important one. But the problem of money always remained.

The staffroom was full by the time Laura arrived. Erika came in, smiling at everyone.

"I need to tell you the latest development with the library books," she said. "I had to tread carefully with the governors. They are justly proud of what we have here at St. Catherine's. Our secondary library is well stocked with textbooks. I spoke at some length, explaining that we need a more diverse selection of fiction and non-fiction. I highlighted the benefits this would have on reading and writing skills and on improving general academic achievements." Erika paused momentarily. "Then I showed them Dulcie's poem, informing them that we have no poetry books at all in lower school. The teacher supplied her own. They were putty in my hands." Erika stopped to smile.

There were murmurs of delight from the staff.

"They have agreed to set aside some funding but we will need to raise the extra money. But all in all, a successful outcome."

This was met with cheers of "well done" and "excellent news". Erika thanked them all and, leaving the staff discussing the implications, she returned to her office.

– – –

The day had been extremely hot, and the surface of the Caribbean Sea was rippling in the threads of whatever breeze was stirring when Laura arrived home. School had been productive with regards to her work with Year Eleven and, of course, the successful feedback from the governors. The air was still very warm and the scent of the frangipani wrapped around her as she went up the steps to her apartment. How beautiful it all was, Laura thought; every morning something new had budded or blossomed in the little garden. She opened the door, and the sun streamed through the windows and welcomed her home. She took a cooling shower and slipped into a sundress before collapsing on her bed. Through the open door she could hear the birds singing, and the sound filled her mind like very peaceful music while she rested.

A gentle tap on the door and Blake announced himself. Laura was delighted to see him; she had become used to him just calling in on her. The apartment was very central and friends were always welcome. For Laura it was one of the joys of Barbados, there was always someone to talk to. All in all, life was taking on a routine that was in itself comforting to her. She ushered him in and Blake sat down on the large sofa among the cushions.

"I've been in New York visiting my parents," he said.

"How was it?" she asked from the kitchen as she prepared coffee.

"Same as usual, tiring and a hassle."

"I meant with your parents," she chided.

"So did I."

Laura smiled. At these times there was an air of confidential understanding between them which Laura valued in a friend. She came through with two coffees and, handing one to Blake, she sat at the end of the sofa and looked at him over the rim of her mug.

"I've brought you something." Blake handed her a flat, circular, whitish object. "I was diving off the reef when I saw it lying there and I thought of you."

Putting her coffee down, Laura looked at it curiously, turning it in her hand.

"What is it?"

"It's a sand dollar, a small sea creature. Alive they're

usually covered in purple or reddish velvety spines. They live for about eight to ten years, and these skeletons lie on the reef."

"It's lovely, Blake, thank you. It feels like coral with five petals and five tiny holes. It looks like a sea star."

"The holes are for feeding," he said, watching her delight.

"I absolutely love it," she said.

Blake regarded her with some amusement. Laura couldn't have been more excited than if he'd given her a precious diamond.

"I know you like to make things from shells, driftwood and stuff." He nodded towards the montage on the wall. "They're works of art, Laura, they really are."

"Well, I wouldn't go that far," she laughed. "But I enjoy making them."

"I guess, Laura, I've always considered art to be for investment. My family buy and sell art. They have agents who look for up-and-coming artists, whose work has the potential to increase in value, or for an artist who could become influential. Their people scour exhibitions, fairs and such like, and my parents usually invest in several artists. They don't necessarily have to like their work."

Laura had been listening carefully, and her eyes creased into an expression of amused disbelief.

"In other words, art is about making money."

"Well, yes, I suppose it is," Blake said.

"Where's the fun in that? I think of art as telling me more about the world, as something I enjoy, but then I'm a just a simple girl."

"No, you're incredible," he said quietly.

Laura realised that the whole concept of beach combing was probably an anathema to Blake, although he had managed to sound interested. In fact, Blake had never thought of collecting such things as driftwood. But then again, he'd never met a girl like Laura, who could get so excited about a sand dollar.

"I just love nature," Laura explained, "especially from the sea. To think such things have been weathered and washed ashore by winds, tides, waves fascinates me."

"I hadn't thought of it like that," Blake admitted. In truth, he hadn't thought about it at all. This was why he always enjoyed Laura's point of view.

"You have a way of making me look at things differently," he said.

Blake was learning so much about Laura, and he had the feeling there was a great deal more to know.

"I guess, I mean, I really like them, they're just…" he hesitated, "well, out of my experience."

Like so many things between us, thought Laura.

"We're from two different worlds," he laughed. For a tantalising moment, Blake wished he belonged in Laura's world.

"You know, Blake, I sometimes think we belong to two different planets." Her eyes twinkled.

"So when shall we go foraging?" he teased.

When something amused him, an impish grin ran through him and Laura felt herself melt inside.

She looked up at Blake; he looked unassailable, but in spite of his grin she thought she caught sight of a raw and painful flicker in his expression – something wasn't right.

"We're friends, aren't we? And friends can speak their minds to one another. Is everything okay, Blake?"

"Not really," he replied. "I went to the Hamptons to see my sister Kristina when I visited New York," his voice was flat.

There was a mystery hanging there, Laura knew it. She guessed it was perhaps the real reason Blake had called to see her, but she remained silent.

"When Kristina was twenty-four years old, she married Steve Trent, who is ten years her senior. Kristina was young and beautiful and Trent a high-flying New York lawyer, from a wealthy family who were friends of my parents. They seemed like the perfect couple, they had the perfect society wedding, the whole nine yards. Yet the memory of that day three years ago fills me with anger!"

Laura was shocked.

"But why?" she asked.

"Because Kristina's journey into hell began on that day. Their marriage is in tatters. Once married, Trent's desire to control everything became more obvious to me. Now Kristina's self-worth and self-esteem are so low. She has no friends up there, she is totally isolated, she never goes out."

"How awful," breathed Laura, "why doesn't she leave?"

"Kristina is in denial. I noticed that he criticises everything she does, but she still thinks she loves him and that she is to blame. I feel guilty because I was never there for her."

"You cannot blame yourself, Blake. You left home and Kristina knows why. What about your parents?"

"That's the worst of it, she says they must not know.

Sometimes I think I should tell them."

"That's tricky. I'm not sure that's a good idea, Blake. She may feel you are taking more control away from her."

"I've even wondered if they would be quite happy for her to stay and keep up appearances, rather than risk a scandal," he added caustically.

Laura shook her head. "You don't know that, Blake," she said.

He exhaled, lowering his head. Blake appeared to bite down on his emotions. Then as he looked up at Laura, she caught a flash of pure anger in his eyes.

"I feel so powerless to help. I don't see Kristina much now, because if he's there I just want…" Blake stopped himself. Laura noticed that he clenched his fists involuntarily.

The edge of anger and sadness to his voice tugged at Laura's heart.

"Kristina must be hurting," she said. "Don't add to it, Blake. Just be there when she needs a friendly ear."

"She used to be so full of life and fun," he said quietly.

"And she will be again, I'm sure." Laura felt the need to be positive. "When the right time comes, she will leave, and you will be there to support her."

Laura gave him hope, she always made him believe things would work out. He didn't have anyone else in his life that did that. Blake felt there could hardly have been a greater contrast between being in New York and being here with Laura.

What Blake had told her horrified Laura. So much was unresolved with his family, she hadn't realised before. He couldn't seem to catch a break. The usually self-assured Blake suddenly looked, to Laura, in deep need of a hug.

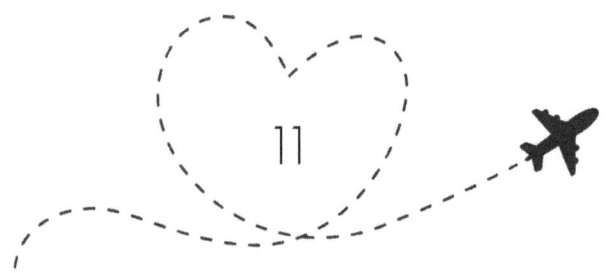

11

Laura was up early and sitting on the veranda drinking tea and soaking in the serene morning atmosphere. Sitting quietly, she watched the tiny hummingbirds hovering over the frangipani and honeysuckle flowers around the balcony and marvelled at their unique ability to fly backwards. Laura felt privileged that they came so close. She liked to think they recognised her. How different it was to Holy Island, where flocks of seagulls would be flying around the beach at this hour, filling the air with their strident squawking, or strutting the beaches as if on guard duty. It was one of life's curiosities that there were no seagulls in Barbados. However, she loved watching the sandpipers, comical little birds that straddled the break-line of the shore and followed the receding waves before quickly turning and running from the incoming tide.

It was St. Patrick's Day, and Laura had recently learnt, to her surprise, that this day was taken very seriously by the people of Barbados, and Carmel was no exception. Today she had invited Emma, Sean and Laura to a celebratory dinner at her home in Paradise Heights.

Ivan was to collect them.

The noise from an engine could be heard. Looking up, Laura saw Ivan's car pull into the courtyard and, as if on cue, Sean appeared around the corner as Emma also emerged from her apartment. Suddenly, the peace was broken. Emma was wearing a tall green hat and greeted them all with, "Top o' the morning."

Sean stared at her, a twinkle in his unblinking green eyes.

"You realise no one in Ireland ever says that."

"Well, they should," replied Emma, "it trips off the tongue."

Getting out of his car, Ivan came towards them. A grin crossed his face when he saw Emma.

"I can't take you seriously in that daft hat," he said, pulling it from her head. Emma laughed self-consciously as she arranged her unruly locks into place. Ivan kissed her on the cheek.

"That's better," he smiled.

"It is," said Emma. "That daft hat is hot and heavy."

Laura collected her bag and chocolates for Carmel and, closing the doors, she headed down the steps to join her friends. Sean was waiting at the bottom.

"I was a bit afraid in case your pilot friend was coming," he said.

"Why?" Laura was taken aback.

"I don't know, I just thought…" he smiled, "forget it."

Laura smiled ironically; Sean obviously still felt there was something between herself and Blake.

"It's okay, Sean, you're safe."

They both laughed; the matter was dropped. It was St. Patrick's Day – a day to have fun.

Arriving in Paradise Heights, Ivan nosed the car into the shade under the carport at the side of his parents' house. Getting out, Laura looked about her. The late morning sun reflected on a neat row of whitewashed villas built on a ridge high above the sea. Opposite, across the road, a tangle of bushes and small trees clustered together on a grassy verge. She breathed in deeply but felt a sense of apprehension. It wasn't lost on her that this was her first visit to Paradise Heights since she left as a three-year-old, and for her there was still a mystery to the place.

Laura followed the others into the house and through to the living room, where Carmel was waiting to welcome them. Kisses and greetings and presents were exchanged.

The soft strumming of a guitar could be heard coming from the terrace.

"Come through," called Marvin. "Welcome, welcome, come and sit."

The garden offered a view down to the sea and Laura noticed it was one of those days when the sea fret hung in sheets along the horizon of the sea, underneath a bright blue sky. They basked in the warmth, the view admired, welcome, cool drinks passed around. Sean and Marvin chanced a Guinness.

"Here's to St. Patrick." Marvin raised his Guinness. The chatting began.

"So, Sean," asked Carmel, "are you from Dublin?"

"No, from Cork, but I lived in Dublin for years. I

trained at Trinity. Spent a lot of time in the Pavilion Bar."

"My family live in Dundrum, just outside Dublin," Carmel told him.

"I know it, but I know Temple Town better," he laughed.

"I'm sure," said Carmel. "The place to find a party after dark."

"It is that," quipped Sean, "the place where more beer is always a good idea. I still miss the craic."

"Are you homesick, Sean?" Carmel asked him.

"At first, when I was on me tod, but since I met your man here," he said, giving Ivan a friendly pat on his back, "I'm happy as Larry."

Laura listened carefully, intrigued by the melodic Irish accents of Carmel and Sean.

"Anyway, thanks for inviting us," Sean said, lifting his glass.

Marvin had been quietly paying attention but was keen to say something now.

"Can I just say a few words?" he asked.

"Do we have a choice?" replied Carmel.

"The Irish have a history with Barbados," Marvin began.

Ivan looked at the others. "I feel one of Dad's lectures coming on," he grinned. He wasn't wrong!

"In the seventeenth century about 50,000 Irish prisoners of war were shipped to Barbados after the Irish clan system was abolished. They became known as the 'Red Legs' because of their easily burnt Celtic skin." He looked directly at Sean, who was sitting there with his easily burnt Celtic skin.

"Wow," said Emma, "who knew?"

"Did you know that, Sean?" Marvin asked.

Sean laughed, "I do now."

If there was more to this discussion, it would have to wait, because Carmel's voice called from inside.

"Ready, come and get it."

They went through to the dining room, where a big table was covered in a white cloth and laid for six people. The meal started out with smoked salmon and potato fishcakes, after which they prepared to devote their energy to the main course. A steaming casserole was placed on the table – this was Carmel's speciality Irish stew, with deep brown, rich gravy and chunks of homemade soda bread. Everyone ate, saying it was delicious. Usually in Barbados Laura ate very little in the afternoon, which was the sensible thing to do in the heat. But today, they all ate for Ireland. Just when Laura thought she couldn't eat another mouthful, out it came: "Guinness chocolate cake," announced Carmel. There were groans all round.

Finally, meal over, they collapsed back on the terrace. The comfortable chairs were heaven to sit back on and relax with a drink. On the plus side, thought Laura, they at least had the rest of the day to recover, and she probably wouldn't need to eat for a week.

The combined effects of a large meal and the warm air slowed down the conversation. Ivan suggested Emma and Sean took a wander down the garden with him, to get a better look at the view. It was at this point that Marvin leaned across to ask Laura how it felt to be in Paradise Heights again.

"Lovely to be here with everyone, but strange at the

same time," she said truthfully.

"How about a visit sometime to the old house you lived in?" Marvin asked kindly.

"I would like that," Laura replied.

"I'll arrange it," said Marvin. Then, changing the subject, he continued, "Sean's a nice fella, I think he likes you, Laura." His eyes twinkled.

"Sean's lovely, but I didn't come here to start something."

"Coming to Barbados is the start of something," replied Marvin.

"In real life it's hard to know when one thing ends and another begins. I mean, I came to revisit the place where I once lived with my parents – I hoped to feel a connection."

"That's natural, of course, but could it be," Marvin said confidentially, knowingly patting his nose with his index finger, "that there's a certain young pilot on this island you really like?"

Laura looked at him questioningly. "How do you know?" she whispered.

"I've eyes in my head," he replied gently.

"My heart isn't ready for a relationship," she said softly.

"If you always try to protect your heart, you will never be happy," he said. "You have to be bold enough to live life, let yourself be vulnerable, be willing to risk getting hurt."

"I've always felt vulnerable, that's the problem."

"Unfortunately, Laura, there are no guarantees in life. Sometimes you have to take a chance."

Laura swallowed hard – she knew he was right.

"It's complicated, Marvin."

"It always is," he replied.

Laura had always liked Marvin but never as much as she did at this moment. Carmel now pulled her chair closer to speak to Laura.

"I spoke to your mother, Rose, a few times. She was lovely, Laura. She lent me a book on tropical plants when I was planning the garden. I got the impression Rose had a book on pretty much everything tucked away somewhere. She told me she had worked in a large bookshop in an old railway station. Had Rose returned I believe we would have become friends."

Laura was both warmed and surprised to find that Carmel had actually spoken to her mother.

"Rose loved Barbados, she acclimatised so well, quicker than she thought. Your father of course loved the tropics, Rose told me. Ever since he did V.S.O. in Dominica he wanted to return to the Caribbean one day."

Laura looked quizzically at Carmel.

"I'm not sure I follow you," she said.

"You didn't know your father was in Dominica?"

"No, I didn't," said Laura.

Carmel wasn't sure what to say. "It's all I can tell you. I hope it helps you to know a little more about your parents, Laura."

Laura was stunned, this was such a strange moment on so many levels. Carmel had spoken to her mother, her father had done V.S.O. in Dominica. The others were now returning to the terrace; Sean was telling a story, and it must have been a good one because Ivan and Emma laughed out loud. It enabled Laura and Carmel to leave the issue.

Night was approaching. The friends sat on the terrace

in Paradise Heights after sharing a wonderful day together. They watched in amusement as the *Jolly Roger* sailed past, laden with its passengers of boozy tourists after a day of fun and games at sea. With its skull and crossbones flag flying high, it was hard to miss. Discordant strains of "Danny Boy" wafted up to the terrace.

"Happy St. Paddy's." Sean raised his Guinness towards the sea and laughed.

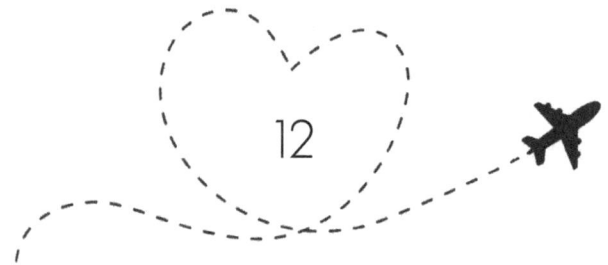

12

Some things had begun to fall into place for Laura since Carmel's revelations on St. Patrick's Day. She now knew that her mother had worked in the bookshop she loved so much. She was comforted by the thought that perhaps her grandmother took her there as a way of reaching out to her as a child, a way of showing her feelings instead of words. Her grandmother was very much old school. That generation were not used to discussing feelings – they were a stoic bunch.

However, learning that her father had done V.S.O. in Dominica now played on her mind. What was the likelihood that Erika had met her father? They were of a similar age and Dominica was a small island. It was a long shot, admittedly, but certainly within the realms of possibility. Discovering anything about her parents had become like completing a jigsaw puzzle for Laura. The tantalising question of Dominica now intrigued her – it was a missing piece. Her instinct was to ask Erika but she wasn't sure.

A shaft of afternoon sun filled the room as the veranda door was pushed gently open and she heard Blake's voice.

"Hey, got time for a break?" he asked.

Waving a hand in welcome, Laura breathed a sigh of relief. She gathered the homework papers together and put them all in a folder to one side of the table. She was more than ready for a distraction.

"Coffee?" she asked as Blake stepped into the room and sank down onto the sofa.

"No, I'm good. I just called in to see you."

Seeing how relaxed Blake was today, Laura thought this might be a good moment to tell him what was on her mind. After all, Erika was a friend of his, so she would never do anything without Blake's blessing.

"I'm glad you're here, Blake, I need to ask you something," she said, turning her chair to face him.

"Fire away," he replied casually.

"I have this need to know more about my parents and I don't think it's going away any time soon."

Blake watched her expectantly. He sensed this was something of importance to Laura; she had become slightly nervous.

"My father did V.S.O. in Dominica, Carmel told me. I know Erika is from Dominica, what if Erika ever met my father? Anything she could tell me, however incidental, would be important to me."

Blake looked directly at her. He saw the hope in her eyes.

"I don't know whether I should speak to Erika?" Laura said. "You know, mixing personal with work. Somehow it seems inappropriate."

Blake put his hand to his brow and pushed back his hair. It was some time before he answered.

"Would you like me to run it past Charlie?" he asked.

"Would you, Blake?"

"Sure," he replied.

"Thank you, I'd appreciate that."

"You got it!" he replied gently. "Now, how about a change of scenery? What do you say we head to the beach house?"

Laura had never been there. For one reason or another, they never got around to it. She was more than a little curious.

"I'd love to," she said, getting up from her chair.

"Give me a minute."

Going through to the bathroom, she splashed water over her face, brushed her hair and, grabbing her bag and posh sunnies, she was ready.

The narrow roads were unfamiliar to Laura as they drove between timber chattel houses, their walls and shutters painted in vibrant pinks, greens and yellows with red pitched corrugated iron roofs above. Wicker chairs and plants huddled on small verandas to the front. On one side wall invariably the ubiquitous satellite dish stared at the sky. Laura had grown to love these houses – they were so much a part of Barbados.

Soon the last glimpse of the chattels was lost as Blake took a left turn and the white sand of a beach spread out in the distance. In spite of it being a beautiful day it managed to rain. The sky darkened as black clouds moved slowly across it and the heavens opened.

"Damn it," said Blake.

"It's not the rainy season. It should be a short and heavy downpour," he told her. Peering between the windscreen wipers, Laura could make out that they were now in some sort of lane. On one side there was open countryside, on the other several large impressive villas. From behind garden walls the "Pride of Barbados" trees could be seen standing tall and proud, their striking red and yellow flowers hanging limp and dripping in the rain.

"It's a bit awkward here," said Blake. "They've been felling a king palm and left pieces of it lying in the road."

"Why would they fell a tree? They're so precious," she asked.

"Because it was hit by lightning weeks ago and it's dead inside. So to prevent it falling down and doing damage to homes or – worse – people, it has to be cut in stages from the top."

"How is that even possible?" asked Laura.

"Believe me, it is. These bits must have fallen off the cherry picker. I hope they're coming back for them when the rain stops."

The beams of the headlights moved across the road as Blake manoeuvred around the remaining logs. Turning, they drove through an open white gate and along a driveway between lush gardens until a guava-coloured building came into view. Blake brought the car to a halt and switched off the engine.

So this was Blake's home. She couldn't see much through the rain but nonetheless she felt a tingle of excitement.

Blake looked at her and shrugged. The rains continued to thunder down. Big drops of water splattered onto the car and slid down the windows, which were now completely steamed up. The last thing Blake had expected was to be caught in a rainstorm with Laura – he'd had other plans. Laura was finding the raindrops strangely comforting. The car was cosy; inside, she felt she was in a bubble of sorts, separated from the world outside. Neither of them were in a hurry to leave.

Hesitating for a moment, Blake turned to meet Laura's eyes. The attraction he felt for her was becoming too strong for him to hold back much longer. He wondered if Laura would ever be ready for anything more than friendship or whether he was banging his head against the wall. Leaning in, he touched his hand gently to her cheek. His heart began beating fast. His slightly parted lips hungrily sought hers. It felt like opening his soul to her.

Laura, too, was wondering about Blake. Those gorgeous, dreamy eyes like deep brown pools now so close to hers. She was falling for him – she wanted that kiss even though it would complicate everything, there would be no going back. The warm feel of his lips against hers stirred a heat within and for a crazy moment nothing else seemed to matter.

Slowly pulling back from him, Laura put her hands to her burning cheeks, aware of the wild racing of her heartbeats.

"It's a big step for me," she whispered.

Blake choked back a sigh; he ached for more than a simple kiss.

"If something feels right…" He left the sentence unfinished. His voice was low and cajoling – his meaning clear.

Laura took a deep breath. She envied Blake's simplistic view.

Blake saw her uncertain expression; he wondered if he'd rushed the chemistry. He touched her arm gently. "It's okay, Laura, no pressure," he said soothingly. "Come on, let's get some coffee."

Getting out of the car, Blake held a jacket over her as they hurried onto the back terrace and into the house. As he was so close to her, the heady mix of rain and her perfume filled his senses and desire jolted through him.

Once inside, the aroma of freshly made coffee wafted towards them as they entered the kitchen. There was the sound of voices coming from the hall; Myrtle, his housekeeper, was talking to someone. There was no time for reflection. Blake stopped short as he realised the beach house had visitors. His mind raced – surely Serena hadn't chosen such a bad time to pitch up.

"Wait here a minute, Laura."

Blake pushed open the door into the hall and closed it behind him. Myrtle came through and adjusted the coffee pot then, giving Laura a knowing smile, she left. Returning a few minutes later, Blake sounded irritated.

"My mother's here," he smiled ruefully. *The best laid plans!* he thought.

She had arrived without prior notice. Laura immediately felt uncomfortable about the whole situation and wanted to leave.

Blake touched her arm.

"Is everything okay between us, Laura?"

Laura smiled and nodded. She knew what he meant but left it.

"What do you want to do, Laura?"

"Leg it," she replied.

Blake chuckled, "Me too, but I think it's a bit late for that."

"Seriously, Blake, I ought to go."

"I would like you to stay," he replied.

"Why would you?" Laura asked, surprised.

"Much as I love my mother, she can be hard work. I would like you to be here. We can never have a conversation without her referring to my single status."

Although she really wished to be as far away as possible before Rhonda Degas made her entry, it was clear to Laura that Blake was in no mood to be alone with his mother tonight. He needed a buffer.

"If you're quite sure," she replied.

Blake exhaled loudly.

"Thanks," he said.

For the first time, Laura saw vulnerability in him. He was showing a completely different side to his personality. His mother had been there less than ten minutes and already Blake was tense.

"I know my mother cares but I wish she wouldn't just arrive unannounced."

Laura understood – there was a fine line between caring and controlling, and it would seem that Blake and his mother disagreed on where it was.

"I could use the moral support." Blake forced a smile.

Blake had learnt that no matter what, Laura had a way of keeping him positive, keeping him calm. Just by being there, Laura made him feel better.

"Okay," she laughed. Now she was fascinated to meet his mother.

In the wake of the downpour steam was rising eerily from the garden, which was now veiled in darkness. The wicker lamps on the terrace cast strange shadows over the corner sofas where Laura and Blake drank coffee and waited. Rhonda appeared, smoothing the creases from her cream silk trousers and top. She certainly didn't fit the matriarchal image Laura had formed of her. Piles of dark hair speckled with silver were swept up at the back of her head. Her features were delicate, her brown eyes expressive. Laura could see she had been a beauty.

Blake had risen to meet her and Rhonda came towards him, arms open to embrace and kiss him.

"I wish you'd told me you were coming," he said, which, to Laura, seemed a perfectly reasonable request.

"It would be nice to see you more often," Rhonda remarked, ignoring Blake's comment.

"I daresay," Blake sighed, "but I'm never sure whether you come to visit or check up on me," he added wryly.

"Nonsense," expostulated Rhonda.

Her manner was curt. She appeared vaguely amused by Blake's response, as if he was behaving like a recalcitrant child, just as she'd expected he would. Rhonda now turned to Laura.

Blake stepped up quickly.

"Mom, I'd like you to meet Laura."

"Pleased to meet you, Mrs Degas," Laura smiled respectfully and held out her hand in welcome.

Rhonda took it limply, looking Laura up and down. There was something about her look which unsettled Laura. It was not so much unfriendly, it was more bemused – her manner was cool.

"You've never mentioned Laura," she addressed Blake.

Rhonda was clearly used to speaking her mind. She didn't seem to see the need to endear herself to anyone. Laura hoped Rhonda hadn't meant to be so impolite when she referred to her as if she weren't there.

"Laura is a good friend," said Blake.

"Ummh, fine." Rhonda seemed disapproving.

Laura saw a shadow pass over Blake's face; she could see the effects of it in his eyes. He was annoyed by his mother's insensitivity.

Laura wanted to say, "We don't need your permission, Rhonda," but held back. Instead, she found herself smiling in amusement. The interaction between Blake and his mother was, to say the least, bizarre.

"Tell me about yourself." Rhonda now faced Laura.

It sounded more like a command to Laura than a friendly get-to-know-you chat. His mother seemed to enjoy being blunt. Sitting back in her chair, she waited imperiously for an answer. There was a pause before Laura felt ready to reply. Rhonda shuffled in her seat, clearly ruffled by Laura's slow response. Laura fully expected Rhonda to say something like, "Hurry up, girl, I'm waiting" and she had to stifle a giggle.

"Not much to tell," she managed to say.

Her reply was non-committal, her body language reflecting her reticence to talk about herself. In truth, Rhonda's condescension had made her bristle. Perhaps she had not fully understood the burden his mother placed on Blake. Laura had realised very quickly that Rhonda Degas was a force to be reckoned with.

"Have you seen Kristina lately, Mom?" Blake asked in a calm tone, which suggested to Laura that he was used to diffusing situations like this.

"I haven't. Kristina and Steve lead such busy lives, she has no time to come to New York."

Blake exchanged a brief, anxious look with Laura. There was a bitter irony here. His mother was oblivious to the truth and he couldn't tell her – Kristina had begged him not to. If ever there was a time Kristina needed a prying mother, this was it.

"Why don't you go to East Hampton, call in on her the way you do on me," Blake quipped, but he was deadly serious.

Rhonda reflected for a moment. "I might just do that."

Rhonda's attention now turned to Blake and the offensive began.

"Isn't it about time you were married, Blake? I should have grandchildren."

Her words hung in the air. Laura saw Blake's demeanour change. He lifted his shoulders in exasperation and inhaled deeply. He'd harboured the forlorn hope that his mother would behave herself in Laura's presence – obviously not. However, he caught Laura's smile and he quickly recovered.

"Who would like a drink? I'm ready for a beer," he said.

"Gin and Dubonnet ice and lemon," requested Rhonda.

"And you, Laura?"

"Rum and Coke, please, Blake."

Blake managed a smile as he brought the drinks. Rhonda was about to say something more but this was a good cue for Blake and he took it.

"My mother is hosting a big gala for charity in New York next week."

"Oh really, which charity?" Laura asked politely.

This miraculously seemed to break the ice and enable Rhonda to show she was a sophisticate. To Blake's surprise the evening started to go smoothly. Rhonda was certainly chair on some important charity committees and they spent some time listening to her talking about her charity work, until Laura decided this could be a good time to sound Rhonda out about something close to her own heart – books.

"Can I suggest a cause you may wish to become involved in, Rhonda?" Laura interjected. "My concern is school libraries. Reading is so vital in education and there is such inequality of access."

"I know nothing about education," Rhonda replied haughtily, as if that were a virtue.

"There is a real need. Some children have never had so much as a picture book. I think you'd be surprised, Rhonda; if you asked in certain areas of New York, for instance, you'd find that some children have no books at all in the home. Research found that in the UK."

"I haven't given it much thought." Rhonda was looking

slightly abashed. This was new territory for her and she was feeling unsure.

"Yes, it's a bit of a Cinderella when it comes to charities," said Laura.

"I must say I don't like to think of little children without even a picture book. That's shocking, but I'm still unsure."

Rhonda cast Blake a quick glance in the hope he would help her out – she had been taken by surprise. Blake had never seen his mother unsure about anything before. He stretched back in his seat and left them to it.

"I believe you are just the right person to get involved. You have contacts and a wealth of fundraising experience. As with any social enterprise it can only come about because people make it happen – people like you, Rhonda."

Rhonda sighed. "It would involve setting up a separate charity, I guess that's possible," she said thoughtfully.

"It wouldn't take a fortune, Rhonda, to fill this need, but what a difference it would make."

Blake watched Laura; she was in her element, she radiated a confident beauty. He was impressed. When it came to something Laura believed in, she was passionate. She'd managed to break through Rhonda's harsh exterior. In one fell swoop Laura had managed to both involve and inspire his mother – no mean feat. He could see Rhonda literally puffing her chest with pride. She would take up the cause – he knew it.

There was noticeably less hostility now. The atmosphere of the evening had shifted to relaxed and polite. The three of them spent some time chatting and drinking, but Laura didn't want to overstay her welcome.

"I must go now," she said, getting up from the sofa.

"I'll come with you," Blake said. "I can ask Rudy to drive us. You'll be okay for a while, Mom?"

"Of course," his mother replied.

Rhonda rose to kiss her goodbye with great gusto, it seemed to Laura. It had almost been an enjoyable evening. Not the one Blake had in mind, that's for sure, but at least he had escaped the attentions of his mother relatively unscathed.

"Thanks, Rudy," said Blake, opening the car door. Laura settled into the back seat with Blake. Rudy put the Mercedes into gear and they set off along the driveway.

"Well, that was interesting," Laura murmured.

Blake grimaced.

"Not the usual response to an evening spent with my mother."

"I noticed Rhonda never mentioned your father once during the entire evening."

"She doesn't see much of him," replied Blake. "My father went to work when I was very young and came home about thirty years later," he quipped.

"Have you ever considered that perhaps your mother behaves as she does because she is lonely?"

"Lonely!" he exclaimed. "No, not at all. Quite the reverse. My mother parties all the time with a cast of thousands. How can she possibly be lonely?"

"That's not the same thing, Blake. You don't have to be alone to have feelings of loneliness."

"Feelings! Now there's something that was never discussed in our family. Growing up, my parents never asked me how I felt. We wouldn't know where to start on that score."

Laura remained silent. That revelation hadn't surprised her at all! It was something they had in common.

"Why am I telling you all this?" Blake looked at her and smiled.

"Because I asked you," she replied.

Once again, Laura had shown him a different point of view. Blake reflected on what she had said and wondered whether possibly, where his mother was concerned, he had been less than perceptive.

"By the way, that was some speech you gave tonight," he said.

"Sorry, Blake, I got carried away."

"No, it's fine. In fact, I'd like to help with the books."

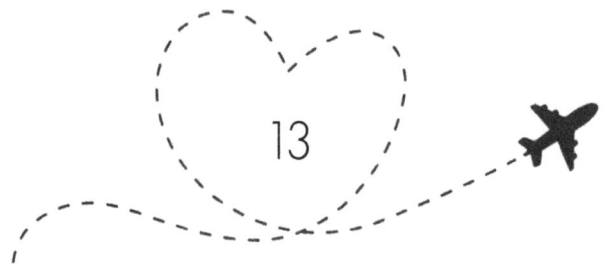

13

Ivan was enjoying the banter with his friend.

"Sherbet lemon springs to mind," he chuckled.

Sean laughed good-naturedly. "You may scoff, but it's the safest colour on the road," he replied.

Nothing was going to dampen Sean's enthusiasm for his newly acquired bright yellow Toyota Aqua. Today was his first day off duty in ten days and he wanted to forget all about the hospital. He had managed to convince Ivan, Emma and Laura to join him on what he blithely described as "a day out" and suggested that they wear long socks, which had Laura totally intrigued. It was right up there with the most random requests ever. Her mind flashed to her wardrobe, which was the antithesis of long socks.

Now here they all were in Sean's Toyota, slowly ascending a narrow road winding up the side of Mount Hillaby in the northern part of the island.

"I've heard the view from the top is stunning," Sean said.

The drive wasn't easy, and as they neared the summit the road became more of a dirt track. Sean ultimately gave up and brought them to a stop on a strip of grass. Leaving the air-conditioned car, they stepped outside to stretch their legs. Thankfully, the warm air hadn't yet reached the full heat of midday. As they gazed down from the towering height, a green hue of vegetation covered the rocks in a series of terraces dropping down to the Atlantic Ocean. Laura marvelled at the way the colours changed as the rays of the sun cast shadows over the scene.

"It must be the most striking view on Barbados," Emma sighed. "It's well worth the drive."

In the distance, Laura could just make out the tiny white building of Cliffside, where Blake had taken her on that special evening with Charlie and Monica. She felt an excited flutter in her stomach.

Sean turned back towards the car and opened the driver's door. He seemed restless – there was something different about him today, Laura could sense it.

"Moving on," he said. "Turner Hall Woods are just north of here. That's the place I really want to explore."

Having grown up on Barbados Ivan knew the area quite well and had a note of caution for Sean.

"The woods are notoriously difficult to find and the road is atrocious. So don't be in a hurry, Sean."

Heeding Ivan's advice, Sean drove slowly and gradually uphill until he suddenly stopped.

"I hate it when that happens," he said.

Ivan looked up. "When what happens?" he asked.

"I've run out of road."

Peering out, they all stared at the mud pile in front of the car.

"This could be tricky," said Sean.

"An understatement. It's impossible," said Ivan.

Others had obviously tried to pass. There were places where the earth had been churned up by the wheels of a vehicle.

"This area is covered in primary rainforest. It was never going to be a walk in the park, Sean," Ivan said.

Sean looked wistful.

"We've got to get in to see it."

"Well, there's a simple solution," Ivan sighed. "We walk from here."

"Really," said Emma dubiously, eyeing the dark woodland ahead.

"Come on, Emma," said Sean coaxingly. "How often do you get the chance to see an ancient rainforest? Where's your sense of adventure?"

Laura looked down at her new socks and walking boots, as yet unused, and made her decision.

"I'm up for it," she smiled.

"Okay, me too," agreed Emma.

Ivan put his arm around Emma's shoulder.

"Are you sure, Em?" he asked kindly.

"I'm sure," she replied.

Breadfruit trees, mahogany and silk cotton trees, as well as a variety of palms, lined each side of a tiny trail, which led them through abundant vegetation. In some places the trees were spaced further apart. As they progressed, an undergrowth of creepers and shrubs created a barrier.

Laura watched anxiously as Sean pushed vines and twigs back with his bare hands like a man possessed, leaving spider webs perilously hanging in mid-air and brushing against their faces. Laura looked up to the canopy of green above. It seemed to reach right up into the clouds. She noticed the boughs touched those of neighbouring trees as they swayed slightly; it was as if the forest was breathing. It was difficult to see daylight, which alarmed her.

"What can we do if we get lost?" she asked.

"Send up a flare," quipped Ivan.

Further in, the forest became greener and more vibrant, and teeming with wildlife. Now and again parakeets took off between the branches, making Laura's heart jump. Curious green monkeys were everywhere, screeching from above. Laura half expected to turn and see a tiger stalking them. She'd no idea before that Barbados could be so feral.

It was jungle and it smelt like jungle. Decaying plants, animal life, trees – the smell filled their lungs.

"This air is thick enough to chew," Emma called from behind.

"And it stinks," added Laura, holding her nose.

Sean breathed in deeply. "The smell of life, it's intoxicating," he said.

He's definitely not right today, thought Laura.

"If you say so, jungle boy." Ivan chuckled.

"Life is a jungle," Sean retorted.

It was hot and humid even in the undergrowth and the route seemed impenetrable, but they trudged on. Finally, they came to a clearing and Ivan called a halt. Exhausted, they all slumped down on a rotting tree stump. Emma was red-faced and puffing.

"You okay, Em?" asked Ivan.

"Peachy," she said, unsmiling. "Do you have your water bottle?" she asked him. Ivan produced a flask of water from his small haversack.

"Always prepared," he smiled.

"Any oxygen in there?" she quipped half seriously.

They each took a swig of the now-tepid water.

"I love it here," said Sean earnestly.

"Are you serious?" Emma asked.

"Being so close to nature fills a deep need in me," he confided.

Laura looked at him, his red cheeks bunching under his eyes, the moisture running down his face. He seemed subdued; he was certainly in a strange mood today. But it was true what he said – she too could feel the energy around her bringing her senses alive. The smells, the sounds, the warm air on her skin, the sense of danger. She loved it.

"At the end of the day, we are part of nature," Sean said.

"I suppose so," Emma agreed. "But it doesn't always feel like it."

Finishing off the water, Emma handed the flask back to Ivan.

"What exactly is it you love so much about being here, Sean?" she asked.

"After the hospital, it's rejuvenating – liberating. Nature is powerful. It's good for our mental wellbeing," he replied.

Ivan put his hand on his friend's shoulder.

"Shit happens, Sean, and often there's no rhyme nor reason to it."

Laura exchanged a quick glance with Emma. Something had happened, they got the message.

"Do you still want to go to Chalky Mount, Sean?" Ivan asked.

"If that's okay with the rest of you?"

"It is," Ivan answered for them. Laura and Emma nodded.

"Can we just sit here a while longer among the chaos?" asked Sean. "I find it very soothing."

It seemed a contradiction to Laura; "soothing" was not the word she would have used. "Frenetic" or "frenzied", perhaps. All the same, she understood Sean. They were sharing an intimate glimpse into nature in all its glory and it was exhilarating. Returning to the car, no one spoke, the experience having left them all in a contemplative mood.

Ivan suggested a longer but easier route that would take them to Chalky Mount – that was if they didn't get lost. Reversing the car to a narrow fork in the road, Sean began the sharp descent. Several kilometres later, Ivan pointed ahead.

"There's Chalky Mount village," he said.

Following the direction of his hand, Laura saw a group of houses come into view, trembling in the heat haze. The village appeared to consist of five or six chattels straddled together on a hillside off the road. Small, dark structures each raised a couple of feet above the ground, allowing the air to circulate. The roofs were the usual corrugated iron and to Laura looked untidy in appearance. In spite of this, she felt the village had a certain attraction.

Sean parked the car under the shade of a large tree and they all got out. Laura could immediately feel the sun coming down on her head like a big bag of hot air. Moving quickly, they made a beeline for a small house with a sign to the front advertising "Banks Beer", and another "Coca-Cola". Sitting in the shade with a cool drink, Laura looked around. The place seemed entirely dedicated to pottery.

"The clay here is a distinctive red colour. It's actually so unique it's exported around the world," Ivan told them.

"Wouldn't that leave big holes in the ground?" suggested Emma.

"It probably does," mused Ivan.

Once again, Sean was on the move. Leaving his drink half-finished, he stood up.

"I can't wait to look over the place," he said.

Strolling across with him, they approached a nearby house with bright green shutters and a veranda out front with an old rocking chair. A woman was standing in the doorway. She smiled at them and beckoned them to come inside. The house was surprisingly cool. A potter was at work on his wheel, around him a long bench full of red clay. In an adjoining room Laura could see shelves were full of pots, jugs, bowls and much more in an array of bright colours.

The potter stopped and waved them over. He introduced himself as Michael and asked if they would like to try their hand on the wheel. Sean moved like lightning. It was clear he was not going to deny himself the pleasures of the potter's wheel. A brief lesson from Michael and Sean was on his own. Laura leant against the wall, standing close to him. As Sean sat down, she noticed his face wore an expression of open, joyous good nature, with a slight shade of embarrassment. Michael threw a lump of red clay onto the wheel and Sean was off.

"Go, Sean," said Emma laughing.

As the wheel span, so Sean began to work the clay, describing the process as though he was talking about a woman. The others smiled as his hands caressed the air and fell back on the clay, working it gently. As he progressed, Laura was impressed to see that it began to resemble a vase, and quite a nicely shaped one at that. The clay had gone a much lighter colour. Sean's grin reached from ear to ear. Eventually, with some reluctance, there was no more work to do and Michael stopped the wheel.

"How beautiful is that?" Sean said, holding up his creation.

"It looks damn good to me," said Ivan.

"This one's for you, Laura, but I'll make one for each of you."

Sean immediately signed up for lessons. Michael took the vase to be fired. Sean would collect it another day.

This odd but wonderful day was coming to an end and Laura had enjoyed every minute of it. Ivan patted his friend on the back as they walked to the car.

"What a day," he said.

"You'll never know how much today has meant to me," Sean said sincerely.

"What's going on, Sean? Can't you tell us?" Laura asked.

Sean turned to look at his friends.

"I lost a patient yesterday. I knew Hector wasn't going to make it, but that didn't help. He had hope in his eyes right up to the end. It really got to me. I've been so angry that life can be so unfair."

Laura saw the anguish in his eyes.

"That's awful Sean," she said. "Why didn't you tell us?"

"I didn't want to lay it on you," he replied.

"It goes with the territory, Sean, get used to it. Getting angry doesn't help anyone." Ivan said brusquely.

"I know. I'm working on it," said Sean flatly. "I realise this is how it's always going to be, like it or not."

"You have to be rational, otherwise you won't be able to do your job," said Ivan.

Ivan is so pragmatic, thought Laura.

"That sounds brutal," said Emma, glancing at Laura, who nodded in agreement.

"It's okay," Sean interjected. "Ivan's right. The other thing I wanted to tell you is that today is my birthday. First one in Barbados. I don't usually celebrate, but today I wanted to be with you guys."

"Happy birthday, Sean." Laura and Emma hugged him.

"Happy birthday, man." Ivan shook his friend's hand. "Look, there'll be many more we can share with you, just not in the jungle," he added.

"Today has made up for so much. Every once in a while I'm reminded how important friends are," said Sean.

"Agreed," said Ivan, putting an arm around Sean's shoulder. "Now, let's get you home before you go all sentimental on us."

- - -

Arriving back at Orient View feeling hot and sticky, Laura was surprised to find Blake waiting for her on the veranda.

"Hey, how you doing? I was just about to leave," he smiled.

Suddenly, Laura was embarrassed. She felt her red cheeks flush even more if that was possible. Blake's gaze fixed on her dishevelled appearance with some amusement. Hair pulled back in a tight ponytail, baggy trousers and tee shirt, muddy boots – she knew she looked like something the cat dragged in.

"I've been in the jungle," she said, feeling the need to give some sort of explanation.

"Attagirl, living the dream," he chuckled.

Ignoring his remark, Laura opened the door. Blake shook his head and, putting his hands in his pockets, he followed her in.

"Charlie's here in Barbados overnight. I had arranged for us to meet up with him later at Fritts Village, but we can do this another time."

"No need, Blake. Just give me ten minutes."

"Only ten?" he mocked.

She shot him a cheeky grin.

In no time at all Laura emerged showered and changed, wearing white, cut-off jeans, sandals and a pale gold top. Her damp hair was swept back behind her ears. Laura gave Blake a smile that made her eyes light up.

"Told you," she said.

Blake smiled back. *God, she's beautiful*, he thought, and his heart turned over.

Soon they reached the tiny restaurant on the beach at Fritts. It was perfect for a low-key catch-up, being quiet and private.

Charlie was waiting for them when they arrived. He greeted Laura with a hug. As she looked into his warm blue eyes, Laura couldn't help but feel she'd known him for much longer than the short time they'd spent together.

"Monica sends her love and asks when you're coming back to Trinidad," he said.

They ordered cool drinks and sat at a little table on the wooden decking over the beach. Pleasantries exchanged, the waiter arrived with the drinks.

"So," began Charlie, not one to beat about the bush, "Blake tells me your father did V.S.O. in Dominica."

"I have only just found that out," she replied.

"I'm curious, Laura, do you have any memories of your father?"

"I have only one," she said simply. "And it begins and ends on Holy Island. My parents happy and smiling. Kissing me and waving as they drove away. I can't recall details of the day – only waiting a long time for them to return – but they didn't. When I awoke the next morning I looked into their bedroom. The suitcases were there, clothes in the wardrobe. They would be coming back soon, I reasoned. Each day I looked the suitcases were still there, the clothes in the wardrobe. Then one day they too had disappeared, the clothes gone. My grandmother became quiet and she no longer smiled. I remember her sobbing. I kept looking, until it finally sunk in I was never going to see them again."

Laura took a deep breath. It was the first time ever she had shared this with anyone and she felt a sense of relief.

Blake and Charlie had been sitting quietly, absorbing her story. There was silence for a moment before Charlie spoke.

"Traumatic," he said quietly.

"Probably why I remember," she sighed.

"No memories before that of living in Barbados?" he asked.

"Not really."

"Well, Laura, here's what we're gonna do. Erika is more than willing to share photos of her V.S.O. friends. She can't remember all of their names, but you may see your father amongst them."

"Thank her for me, Charlie."

"I suggest we arrange to get together at the house. Bring any photographs you have. Erika may recognise him. It was a long time ago, and she doesn't want you to get your hopes up."

"I won't," she said. But she already had.

"Sound good?" Charlie asked gently.

"It does," replied Laura.

"Let's see what, if anything, comes of it," said Charlie.

"Thanks."

"No worries," he said. "That's what friends are for." Charlie put his drink down on the table and leant back in his seat. "I have some news of my own I want to share with you – Monica is pregnant. We are expecting our first child." Pleasure and pride spread over his face.

Laura leaned over to kiss him on the cheek.

"That's wonderful, Charlie, give my love and best wishes to Monica."

"Congratulations, this calls for a celebration," said Blake. "How about we stay here to eat? The pasta is homemade and is supposed to be very good. And what's more, we get to choose our own food, no Monica," he teased.

Charlie laughed. "I'm up for it."

"Laura?" Blake looked questioningly at her.

The need she felt to give and not take rose again in her mind. "Yes, but I would like it to be my treat."

"No way," said Blake. "I've got this."

"No, really, I insist," said Laura.

They sat for a long time, eating and talking in the little restaurant. Laura found Blake and Charlie to be such easy company. Darkness fell and the coloured lights along the roof line came on, casting a warm glow across the sands. Eventually, the waiter came out to wipe down the empty tables and collect glasses, leaving the three of them to stay as long as they wanted.

Laura's mind roamed over the events of the day. Something was changing inside her, she could feel it. *There are critical moments in life,* she considered, *and they can feel like a crossroads.* Today had been full of such moments.

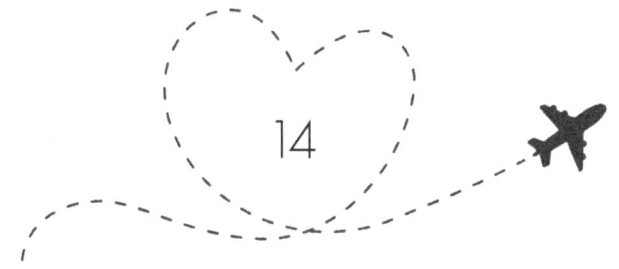

14

It was the day of the first ever St. Catherine's school fair, organised by a committee from the P.T.A. Posters advertising the event "A Community Affair" had been circulated to shops and markets and it was hoped there would be a good turnout. In a few weeks' time, the academic year was coming to a close. Exams were over and school holidays approached. Everyone at St. Catherine's was in celebratory mood. An entrance fee of Bds$10 covered everything and funds raised were to be set aside for school library books. Most importantly, for teachers and parents alike, it had to run like clockwork yet provide a fun day for all. Laura felt happy to be part of it.

Arriving in good time, Laura could hear organ music carried lightly on the air and noticed a carousel spinning slowly in the middle of the school field. Women in bright clothing, their straw hats flapping as they bent, were patiently putting up trestle tables and covering them with colourful cloths. Liam and Zach the caretaker were adding the finishing touches to a long frame with canvas on top to keep the direct sunlight off the heads of those wishing to try their luck on the coconut shy. Several pupils were helping to hang a heavy blanket along the back. A small group of parents gathered around a canvas tent, attempting to get it up and stable. Rows of flags and balloons dangled everywhere, adding to the buzz of excitement.

Turning on to the terrace, Laura was met by a sea of earnest faces. A group of her Year Ten and Eleven students had volunteered to run their own stalls and to generally help out in any way they could.

"Have you got everything you need?" Laura asked.

"I think so," replied Carl in a muffled voice from behind a big box he was carrying. It was full of sweets, notepads, shampoos and so on, kindly donated by his parents from their general store. They were to be used for prizes in the lucky dip bin. Carina had a knobbly looking linen bag over her shoulder, which rattled as she walked.

"Seashells for our lucky shell table," she explained.

Her best friend, Dara, carried a blue cloth, which she held up to show Laura.

"Blue for the sea," she said cheerily.

"Mm, very clever," grinned Laura.

Jaden followed at the rear with two camp stools under his arms.

"Carina and Dara say they can't do without them," he explained, as he struggled to keep them stable.

Laura smiled, touched by their eagerness. She reflected on how fond she had become of her pupils, how much she would miss them, and her mind clouded momentarily. She felt truly happy here in Barbados. Life was good. However, there was a decision looming – to stay or return to Holy Island. But for the moment, that would have to wait.

Laura understood very little of the chatter going on around her as the youngsters set up their stalls. Glancing around, she could see mums talking and laughing at the lemonade stand. Their lemonade was advertised as being made of fresh limes, which puzzled Laura, and she was determined to try some before the day was over. There was a cake stand, cotton candy, trays of fortune cookies and Emma was in charge of face painting. At the far end, a goal post with a hole in the net had been securely fixed for a penalty competition. How many goals scored in four minutes? Despite the strangeness of many things on the field, Laura thought it looked for all the world like a bona fide fairground.

Leaving them to it, Laura headed to the staffroom, now turned into a tearoom, providing a haven for those wanting a rest and a cup of tea. As she passed along the terrace, the school cooks were setting up a food station in-keeping with the theme of the day. The wonderful aromas of Bajan fishcakes, Indian curries and Chinese fried rice wafted into the air.

Laura sat quietly, thinking about her life between the two islands, mulling over her options. Erika had offered her a permanent contract and asked her to give it serious thought. Most of the time, there was no doubt in her mind. She loved her life here, day after day of warm sunshine, good friends and colleagues. She often thought that if she hadn't come to Barbados she would never have known how much happiness was out there waiting for her. She had history with the island. It was here that she had lived with her parents and the connection was important to her. Then there was Blake. The chemistry between them was undeniable but their backgrounds set them apart. Stepping into Blake's world was a whole different ball game, and she didn't know how she felt. On the other hand, Holy Island offered her security and familiarity. Her grandmother had left the cottage to her in her will. The legalities were not yet finalised, usually taking more than six months. She also wanted to catch up with David. They hadn't been in regular contact since she arrived in Barbados, but theirs was an old friendship that didn't rely on constant communication. These thoughts swirled around in her head.

Visitors now started to pour onto the field. Groups of adults stood chatting. Children waved at each other; leaving their parents, they were free to roam. The field became scattered with bright colours. Stalls were getting busy. It was turning into a noisy, enjoyable occasion.

Laura returned to the field to check on raffle ticket sales and collect some of the takings to give to the school secretary. As she passed a small tent, a voice called out to her.

"Hi there, Laura."

She couldn't see the figure clearly – she had a scarf around her head with beads hanging like a fringe above her eyes, but she knew the voice. It was the school secretary, looking every inch the fortune teller.

"Pop by later, I'll tell your fortune," she called.

If only, thought Laura.

"I might take you up on that," she called back, smiling.

Charlie arrived as she was counting money. He came behind her and put his hands on her shoulder.

"Can we talk later?" he asked.

"Of course. We can meet in the staffroom after the fair."

"Sure," he said. He turned to go.

"Charlie, if you want some excitement, Ivan's down at the penalty shootout, pretending he's sporty." She pointed towards the goal post now surrounded by a small crowd, cheering each time a goal was scored. Charlie waved in acknowledgement and headed off.

As it neared four, it was getting almost too hot for any activity. The air was still and oppressive, and the school field smelt of heat and food. Laura could feel her energy beginning to flag. It was time to start packing away. Emma, Aylen and Dulcie came to find her. They had finished the face painting. Dulcie's face was painted with whiskers and eyes like a lion. She held her hands up in front of her and pretended to roar.

"Looking fierce, Dulcie," smiled Laura.

Charlie and Ivan now returned together with red, flushed faces and dishevelled hair. They'd been kicking balls in competition with some of the boys from St. Catherine's football team. By the looks of them, they had come off worse. Excusing themselves, they went off to find refreshments.

At that moment, Erika came out to the terrace. Taking the microphone, she began to call the raffle winners to the crowd gathered in front of her. Afterwards, she thanked the P.T.A. for their hard work, and everyone who came to support the fair and make it a success. The amount finally raised would be printed in the school magazine. There was much applause. Gradually, everyone began to leave. The field went quiet. The music stopped. The school fair was over.

Laura heaved a sigh of relief – all had gone well. She began to walk with the others to meet Charlie and Ivan. Suddenly, Dulcie stopped and complained of feeling unwell. Her breath became hoarse and difficult. Aylen looked in alarm at Emma and Laura.

"What is it?" asked Emma, seeing Dulcie beginning to struggle for breath. Even under the paint, Laura could see that Dulcie's face had grown almost purple as she gasped, clenching her fists in the air. She seemed on the point of choking.

"Has she eaten something?" asked Laura, looking on in horror.

"No," said Emma.

"Dulcie," cried Aylen, despair written on her face as she held Dulcie in her arms.

"I'll find Ivan," said Laura. "You wait here, Emma."

"Hurry, please," Emma called after her.

Dulcie was now fighting the air with her helpless little hands.

In what seemed like a lifetime but was only a minute or two, Emma saw Ivan hurrying towards them – bag in hand. He was accompanied by Charlie.

"Oh, blessed moment," she whispered.

"Can you sit up a little for me, Dulcie?" The calm voice of Ivan seemed to placate her. Ivan quickly dispensed a cool mist humidifier which cooled her down, and her breathing became less laboured.

"What was it?" Emma asked.

"It could be several things, even a viral infection. I'll take her to A&E in my car."

"If you get the car, Ivan, I can carry Dulcie," said Charlie, lifting a limp Dulcie into his arms.

Ivan hurried to bring the car round to the front of the school building. Aylen got into the back seat and Charlie put Dulcie carefully beside her. Emma jumped quickly into the front.

"Please let Dulcie be alright," murmured Laura under her breath as she stood with Charlie and watched them drive away.

"She's in good hands," said Charlie. He put his hand on Laura's shoulder. "Come on, I'll drive you home. I'm guessing you could use a drink."

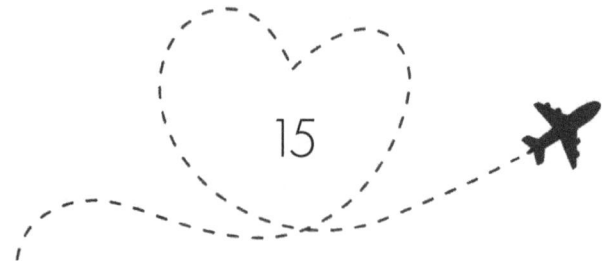

15

A week had passed since the school fair. Laura and Sean strolled along the beach towards the market. The night was warm and drowsy, the air heavy with the tempting smell of fish cooking. As they got nearer, they could hear the soft crackling of flames and see skewers of fish lying across a charcoal barbecue on a boat. Marc and Aylen greeted them warmly as Sean handed over the cold beers and Pinot Grigio they had brought.

"Wa' goin' on? We got rum punch," laughed Marc, adding their bottles to the many others at the bar. Ivan and Emma waved a hello, Emma patting the seat next to her, inviting Laura to come and sit.

"Boy, this is going to be a good night," said Sean.

Tonight was a special thank-you to Sean and Ivan, who had watched over Dulcie during her five days in hospital with breathing problems. Aylen and Marc had Dulcie late in life and she was their world. They wanted to show their gratitude.

Aylen had gone to town with the preparations. A large table was laid with a white cloth and filled with dishes of salad, baked breadfruit, macaroni pie, peas and rice, plus a dish of fresh oysters. At one end a big bowl of fruit, including mango, guava and pineapple, sat alongside a platter of freshly baked bright pink coconut sugar cakes and a tall jug of watermelon crush. Aylen and Marc had delivered a feast for them.

"This is so cool," said Sean enthusiastically. "As good as Oistin's restaurants any day."

Laura smiled. Sean had a way of being excited about everything as if he'd just been let loose for the first time. She loved that about him.

Dulcie appeared in her pyjamas to say hi to everyone. She beamed delightedly but said nothing.

"Off to shuteye with Dada," Aylen told her, gesturing with her hand.

Dulcie waved obediently and left reluctantly with Grandpa Fidel. Aylen was taking no chances, Dulcie still needed plenty of rest.

"I'd never heard of RSV," said Laura, blowing a goodnight to Dulcie.

"Nor me," agreed Emma.

"Respiratory syncytial virus," said Sean. "It's actually a very common infection, especially in children. It affects the upper airways and lungs and can lead to bronchitis or even pneumonia. We can treat the symptoms in hospital. Then it's usually a couple of weeks at home with rest and plenty of fluids before full recovery."

Sean was hardly ever serious – not really serious.

Laura always had that feeling he was winding you up. But when he really cared about what he's saying his voice was different – quiet – like now.

"She gud now," said Aylen, giving Sean a hug; she was pretty close to tears. It was touching to see. Then, wiping her eyes, she began passing around white dinner plates.

Marc brought out flying fish, red snapper and swordfish, all beautifully done. The food tasted as good as it looked. They ate and drank and talked and ate and drank some more.

"What yu bin up to?" Marc asked Sean.

"Well, today Laura and I have been on the sugar train up to Cherry Tree Hill."

"The steam locomotive?" asked Ivan.

"The very same. It runs on a very narrow gauge. We visited the seventeenth-century plantation house."

"Thankfully Dad's not here or we'd be getting a full history lesson now," laughed Ivan.

"There's a cultural centre there dedicated to the history of the area," said Laura. "It would make a good school trip. I think it's important to know the story of Barbados."

There were serious nods of agreement all around.

However, for some reason, Aylen's mind was not on history. She had another take on what she'd just heard, one more of a social nature.

"Sean, he gud-lookin', yu gud together. Yu goin' out wit he, Laura?" she asked.

The question had hardly left her lips when, at the far end of the table, Emma was shaking her head at Aylen. Laura took a deep breath. Aylen was only trying to match her and Sean.

"We're good friends, aren't we, Sean?" Laura knew it was beginning to sound like a mantra. So many people seemed interested in her love life. She wasn't used to this.

"We are that," Sean smiled. Taking a swig of his beer, he looked the picture of restraint.

"I got dat all wrong?" asked Aylen. "Yu not together?"

"'Fraid not," smiled Sean. "But it doesn't mean we can't enjoy each other's company."

Looking at them both intently, Aylen wanted more. Emma tried to throw a rapid glance at her, to no avail. There was no stopping Aylen, she was on a roll.

"So, who de boyfriend?" she asked Laura.

Emma groaned. Ivan chuckled to himself. Then there was silence.

"There isn't one at the moment," replied Laura quietly.

"You gawh be kiddin'!" exclaimed Aylen.

Could things get any worse? wondered Emma, knowing how private Laura liked to be. Well, yes, of course they could, knowing Aylen.

"Dat pilot – he cum by yu back door but yu not sexing wit he?" Aylen looked at Laura with surprise, waiting.

"AYLEN!" Emma almost shrieked, burying her head in her hands.

"No, we're just friends," repeated Laura. She began to see the funny side and a fluttering sensation started in her stomach.

Emma looked up in astonishment.

"How do you even know about Blake?" she asked.

Aylen did that typical Bajan thing: she pointed her finger at her nose to suggest she had a secret to keep.

Sean put his hands behind his head and leaned back languidly.

"What can I say, Laura, it's usually my sex life that's up for discussion." He spoke without the least trace of embarrassment but with pure mischief in his eyes.

"You haven't got one," Ivan piped up.

"A mere detail," Sean replied.

"So dem oysters no damn gud," said Aylen solemnly.

Sean began to laugh. A quivering sensation reached Laura's throat and she failed to suppress a burst of laughter. Suddenly, they were all laughing, really laughing – belly laughing – taking deep breaths. Then Marc stood up and turned on the music.

"Cumma, we gotta party," he said.

Aylen began to clear the table and put leftover food into the fridge. Emma was first up to dance; she seemed to float onto the sand. Aylen came out from the back, swaying her hips and moving her hands in the air. Sean put his hand out to Laura.

"Allow me," he laughed.

"I'm feeling a bit lightheaded," said Laura.

"Good, no one should dance sober," said Sean. "You can't dance when you're self-conscious."

"Is that your professional opinion?" she asked.

"It is. Come on, let your hair down."

Moments later, everyone was on the beach, dancing, moving their bodies in time to the beat of the music. Whirling around joyfully, twirling in the sand. Faces animated, hair flapping around their shoulders. Dancing in the dark on the sand between the sea and the fire in the boat. For Laura, there was something medieval about it all. It was both intimate and liberating. It was a beautiful feeling.

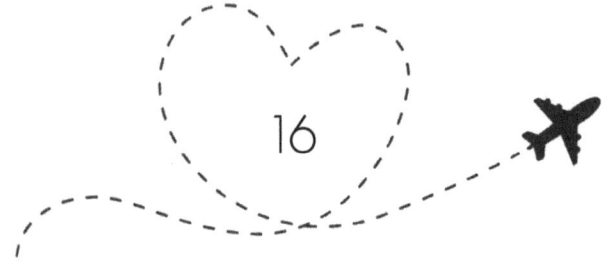

16

Laura woke up early despite having gone late to bed and having slept very little. Marvin had not forgotten about Paradise Heights, as she guessed he wouldn't. The day of the visit had arrived and Laura's resolve began to weaken; she began to doubt the wisdom of what she was about to do. It had seemed like a good idea to revisit the house – connecting with her past was a big part of the reason for coming to Barbados in the first place. Yet the reality felt deeper and more personal. Tension was building up inside her. Resting her face in her hands, she breathed through her mouth as she tried to relax. Marvin had kindly arranged today with the very best of intentions and Laura didn't want him to think she was ungrateful, she wasn't, but she was emotional.

Everything about the day seemed normal, but for Laura, what she was about to do was of great significance. She remembered little of her early childhood. Her grandmother never broached the subject and she learnt from an early age not to ask questions. All these years later, to enter the house where she once lived with her parents was a pivotal step for her. Composing herself as best she could, she was ready and waiting when she heard Blake's car arrive in the courtyard. There was no going back.

It was a glorious day as they arrived in Paradise Heights. Small, puffy, white clouds dotted the blue Caribbean sky. Blake parked in the shadow of a clump of paw-paw trees, their green and yellow fruit hanging down in bunches between the leaves. Underneath, two green monkeys sat gazing at them.

As Laura and Blake left the car Marvin greeted them warmly and they walked with him in the sunshine to a modest detached villa. Marvin was in good spirits, although Laura suspected he was trying to help her feel more at ease.

"Take as long as you want, Laura, the owner knows the importance of your visit," he said kindly before taking his leave. Now alone with Blake, Laura was aware of a tight knot gripping her stomach.

"Are you okay, Laura?" Blake asked.

"I'm trying to be," she said. "I don't feel…" The rest of the sentence drifted into the air as the front door opened before they had even reached it and a smiling, middle-aged Bajan lady welcomed them in.

Going into the entrance hall, Laura took a deep breath to try to calm her nerves. She hadn't taken more than two steps when she stopped. It was the smell! The faint scent of lemongrass from the polished wood flooring immediately evoked memories of her childhood. Momentarily, she felt an overwhelming sense of loss. Feeling uncertain, she hesitated for a moment before entering a large, bright room.

Looking around, she took it all in. It was a pleasant room, simply furnished with a brown sofa and two matching armchairs. Smart plantation shutters at the window gave shade from the sun and a glass chandelier hung from a high, white ceiling. It all felt strange to Laura. She was finding it difficult to imagine that she had spent so much time in this house. Curiosity now soothed her anxiety as she passed slowly along a short passage and through an open door into a bedroom. A large bed lay between two windows. A dressing table stood at one end of the room and a mahogany wardrobe at the other. A vaulted ceiling gave the impression of space. An open window let in a cooling breeze, which blew the long, white, voile curtains to and fro around the bed in an almost ghostly way. Nonetheless, there were no ghosts here; the home felt loved and tranquil. The windows offered a brief glimpse of a small, lawned area outside. Laura's memory cast back to one of her mother's cards, the words echoing through her mind.

"Today we bought Laura a small paddling pool for the garden. She splashes around in the water, giggling. We love to hear her laugh. She gives us so much joy."

Laura felt a surge of emotion and had to fight back the tears. She couldn't help thinking of her parents. As much as they loved her as a child, they would never know her as an adult.

The terrace opened up to the view of the garden and

Laura could see down to the turquoise sea and hear the reassuring rhythm of the waves. Stepping outside, she looked across the patio and there it was! The old breadfruit tree looking almost exactly the same as in her treasured photograph. Shadows of her childhood crowded her mind as her eyes followed the contour of its thick brown girth up to the canopy of leaves and golden fruit above. The blue sky dappled between the branches. Slowly, she walked towards it and reached out to touch the gnarled bark, running her fingers up and down to feel the texture. Leaning her head lovingly against it, she stretched her arms around the trunk. She found it hard to believe that this beautiful old tree had come to represent a timeless memory for her. The leaves gently rustled as though sharing her loss. Closing her eyes for a fleeting moment, Laura had a sensation of happiness with her parents, a feeling so personal it could never be shared or put into words. Blake stood back, not wanting to intrude on this very private experience for Laura.

The poignancy of the afternoon had been intense for Laura and as Blake drove her home they were both caught up in their own thoughts. Late afternoon they arrived back at Orient View. Blake sensed that Laura wanted to be alone. He regarded her with some concern.

"I don't like to leave you," he said.

Laura blinked as if suddenly coming to. She gave him an apologetic smile.

"Thank you, Blake, but I just need…" Her voice trailed away and her legs felt weak as she hurried out of the car. Blake breathed in a deep sigh and nodded.

Pent-up emotional energy racked Laura's body and, as much as she tried to hide it, she was close to bursting into tears. Going directly to her bedroom, she changed into her swimsuit, and grabbing a towel and cover-up, she headed straight to the beach. Desperately needing to do something physical to ease the tension now stiffening her body, she waded into the sea and began to swim. The warm Caribbean waters washed over her soothingly, giving relief, and soon the pain in her diminished. The beach was deserted and leaving the water, she walked towards the sea grape tree where she'd left her things. She was fond of sitting here – it was peaceful and private and had become a sort of refuge. Spreading her towel in its shadow, Laura lay down.

After a while, she became conscious of a movement nearby, emerging from the line of breadfruit trees at the edge of the little gardens. Squinting through the stippled sunlight, she caught her breath in surprise. It was Blake.

"I just came back to check on you because I fly out early tomorrow morning. How are you holding up?"

Laura smiled at him. She gave no answer, but the steady reassurance of his voice comforted her. Removing his top, Blake sat down beside her to enjoy the late afternoon sun. They listened to the swishing of the waves and watched the tiny crabs that darted in and out of the rising tide. Laura looked at Blake; there was a stillness about him. Today he had shown her glimpses of a warm and complex personality.

"I was overpowered by sadness today," Laura said quietly. "The time I spent with my parents was so fleeting.

But being in the house for the first time, it felt real. My parents did exist, we were together once in the house at Paradise Heights. I'm not that little girl anymore but so much trauma in my early life was unresolved. It can sort of bend you out of shape. I realise I cannot change the past – I have to accept it, with all its limitations."

Blake's heart went out to her. He marvelled that she could be so philosophical. How much he admired her.

"Sometimes, Laura, you have to push some thoughts to the back of your mind. Let go of what you can't change so you can get on with your life."

Laura guessed Blake was speaking from experience. She knew he was beginning to break through the protective walls she had built around herself.

Stretching out on the towel, Laura could feel the warmth of the white sand beneath. Breathing in deeply, the fresh sea air filled her lungs.

"I love it here," she sighed wistfully. "I could stay forever."

Blake looked at her as she lay beside him, her eyes closed. Beads of water caught the light and sparkled in the sun from her wet hair falling around her breasts. The need to touch her, to be touched by her, to make love to her, now rushed through him. He moved closer, slowly sliding the straps of her swimsuit off her shoulders. His fingers brushed her cheek and moved dreamily down the curve of her face, stroking her neck and coming to rest on her breasts, still cool and silken from her swim. His touch lingered there, gently caressing her.

Laura could feel his warm skin against hers – the

scent of him filled her every breath. She moaned softly. A smouldering sensation spread through her whole being and her pulse began to race. Desire was swelling inside her like the waves of the incoming tide.

"Laura." His voice was soft and sensual.

She turned to look at him and felt herself falling into those dark eyes, now fuelled with emotion. Reaching up, she put her arms around his neck and tilted her face towards him. Blake lowered his head and his warm lips closed over hers. It was the moment both had longed for. On that beautiful afternoon in Barbados, Laura gave herself to Blake in a way she had never done to anyone before.

Afterwards, they lay there together on the beach, both stunned by the heated passion that had flowed from each of them. Darkness fell, and the birds began their evensong. Bats flapped their wings as they flew out of the shadowy corners of the gardens along the shoreline. Laura looked up at the night sky, the stars glittering onto this special moment. Tears misted her eyes; a million thoughts flooded her mind. She could no longer dismiss the emotion churning within her. The truth was simple. She was in love with Blake Degas.

Early the next morning in Orient View, Blake prepared to leave. He kissed Laura lightly on the forehead as she lay in bed. Laura reflected on how far she had come since arriving in Barbados, burdened with her emotional baggage. Blake had helped her through so much. He had shown that he could be empathetic and nurturing. He made her feel important to him, showed that he cared for her. Heaven knows she had tried to resist him, but this felt different. Laura wanted to tell Blake what was in her heart, but she could never bring herself to say it aloud – until now.

"I love you, Blake," she said softly.

Blake didn't respond. Laura looked anxiously up at him. She wanted to tell him again but she couldn't, self-doubt took over. She could see even in the dim light of the bedroom that Blake looked as though he wanted to say something but changed his mind.

Blake felt something dark well up from within – a physical thing, a sort of fear. He turned to go; he had to get to the beach house to change. He had a flight; he was the captain. There was no time to talk about anything. Stopping in the doorway, he took one last look at Laura, a solemn stare as if seeing her for the first time. Then he left abruptly, trying to fend off the feeling.

Laura heard the veranda door open and close and Blake's car backing out of the courtyard. He was gone. She looked at the bedside clock: it was five am. Laura felt herself trembling, unable to make sense of what just happened. She knew for certain that Blake's demeanour was different. She could not forget that look in his eyes.

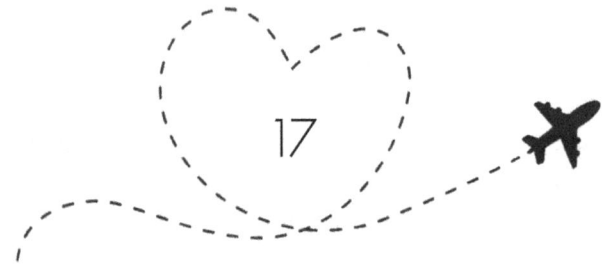

17

Looking out of the car window, Laura watched as the sun sank low in the sky and the calm Caribbean waters glistened in the fading light. Charlie was taking her to see Erika in the hope that she may recognise her father from his time in Dominica. Her mood was low. She was still trying to make sense of what had happened with Blake a few days ago. She thought that they had a real connection. Now she was unsure. The chill she felt in her heart mingled with butterflies of anticipation in her stomach, making her feel nauseous.

Charlie pulled up outside a modest brick house on the outskirts of St. Michael's district. Erika opened the door to greet them as they walked up the drive; she looked happy to see them. Hugging Laura warmly, she led them into a spacious lounge. The room exuded elegance. A luxuriously piled Indian rug in shades of blue graced a terracotta-stone flagged floor. Two dark blue sofas were arranged each side of a large glass-topped coffee table. To one side of the room, a teak sideboard displayed photographs alongside a bright orange Bird of Paradise plant. Laura and Charlie made themselves comfortable on one of the sofas. Liam breezed in from the adjoining kitchen.

"Lovely to see you, Laura, coffee? Tea? Cool drink?"

"Coke for me, please, Liam."

"With ice?"

"Please."

"I'll have the same, Liam," said Charlie.

"Are you okay, Laura?" Charlie asked. "You look a bit tense."

"I'm okay, thanks, Charlie."

Liam returned with the drinks, pulling up a small side table to put them down in front of Laura and Charlie.

At this point, Erika was still searching through a cupboard in the sideboard. Taking out several photo albums, she put them to one side on the floor.

"Photo albums, such a thing of the past," she laughed. "I'm hoping I can help you, Laura," she called. Erika was still on her knees, rummaging through the sideboard cupboard.

"Let's relax first, Mum," said Charlie. "Come and join us."

"Good idea," agreed Liam.

He'd been watching Erika carefully. He was not the only one – it was becoming clear to them all that she was a little on edge.

"Erika has prepared sandwiches and a cake. Her lemon cake is to die for, Laura," said Liam.

An unfortunate turn of phrase, Laura felt, but she knew Liam was trying to create a relaxed atmosphere.

"Sounds lovely, thank you," she said.

"I'll help you, Liam," said Charlie, getting up and leaving with him.

Laura was feeling a little uncomfortable. She knew she was impinging on Erika and Charlie's kindness.

"I'm sorry to have intruded like this, Erika," she said.

She was about to elaborate and tell her how much it meant to her, when Erika interjected.

"Please don't be sorry, Laura. I haven't looked through these albums for years. It gives me an opportunity to reminisce about my youth, which I am quite excited about," she said graciously.

At this point, Charlie and Liam returned with tea, sandwiches and lemon cake, as well as four white plates and napkins.

"Please help yourselves," said Liam, putting the tray on the coffee table.

Laura took a piece of cake as Liam poured tea for them. They relaxed and chatted. They discussed the school fair, Charlie and Monica's good news and how much they were looking forward to being grandparents. The lightness of the evening contrasted profoundly with the reason for Laura's visit. Before she knew it an hour had passed. Liam got up.

"Right, well, I'll leave you to it," he said as he turned to go. "Good luck," he added, smiling at Laura.

Erika now came to sit opposite Laura and Charlie. She put her tea on the table to one side.

"Would you like to look through this book, Laura? I think it's a good place to start."

She handed Laura a thick brown album.

"I must say I don't recall meeting anyone from the north of England, or anyone with the surname Stevens," she said softly.

Laura wasn't really listening, she was engrossed in carefully searching every face on the pages in front of her. In the meantime, Charlie and Erika continued to sip tea and discuss Monica's pregnancy. The mood was mellow.

Then, like many critical moments in life, it all seemed to happen quickly and unexpectedly. Laura's attention was suddenly drawn to a young man in a group photograph. Casually dressed in shorts and a tee shirt, the man posed against the backdrop of mountains. The same young man popped up in several other photographs. Laura turned the pages back and forth to look again at the same individual. Faces change, she thought, but the eyes are a giveaway. They always show the person inside, and Laura could see her father's eyes looking back at her from the page. Her throat tightened, and it took a while to sink in. She looked up; Charlie and Erika were chatting and drinking tea. The atmosphere was relaxed, contrasting with the turbulence that was now going on in her mind. She closed her eyes for a moment and took a few calming breaths before she whispered.

"This is my father, Erika."

"Where?" asked Erika excitedly, turning towards her. Charlie tilted his head to take a look. Handing the album to Erika, Laura pointed to the young man. A moment of happiness on Erika's face quickly turned to a sad, nostalgic smile.

"Are you sure?" she asked.

"There is no doubt in my mind," replied Laura.

"I'm baffled," said Erika. "This young man is from Plymouth and his name is not Stevens."

"I am sorry, Erika. I have gone about it all the wrong way. I was so intent on searching through your albums I neglected to explain something to you. My grandmother was given legal guardianship when my parents died and I have always been known as Laura Stevens, which is my grandmother's surname."

Laura opened the manilla envelope and took out the faded photograph of her father and gave it to Erika. Sitting back on the sofa, Erika stared at the photo in her hand. There was silence for a moment.

"My father was John Kavanagh," said Laura softly.

Charlie inhaled expectantly. In a single heartbeat everything changed.

"John Kavanagh is Charlie's father," said Erika, her voice unsteady. She looked at Charlie, shock in her eyes.

"It's okay, Mum," he said, pressing a hand onto her shoulder. She reached up to place her hand over his. Her eyes filled with tears and they rolled down her cheeks.

"So John has been dead for years?" said Erika sadly. "I'm sad John never knew you, Charlie. I always had hope that perhaps one day... He didn't get to see you grow up, Laura." Erika wiped the tears from her eyes. "Death is so final, I'm just sad." She stretched her hand across the table and placed it on Laura's. She smiled gently. "Thank you, Laura, now I know."

"You're my sister – my blood, my family," said Charlie.

A lump formed in Laura's throat. She loved him for saying that.

"I don't remember much at all about my parents," said Laura.

"I'd like to share some of my memories with you both," replied Erika. "Charlie may have already heard most of them."

"I'd like to hear them again – share them with Laura," said Charlie.

Laura browsed through the albums as Erika shared her stories, snippets and morsels that she thought she would never hear.

"I met John when he was fresh out of university. He was handsome – wonderful blue eyes, dark hair. I had just qualified as a teacher. We met at a party and spent the night talking. As you know, the geography of Dominica makes it prone to natural hazards. John was working with V.S.O. on projects such as hurricane risk, population movement. He came into school to give a talk on the work. We had a wonderful affair but it ended before he left. I was never able to trace him to tell him I was pregnant; it was difficult in those days. Then life takes over and you just get on with it. When Charlie was born it was the best day of my life." She began to smile – it was an expression that seemed to radiate from deep within her, yet she struggled with tears again.

"Looking at these pictures, Erika," said Laura, "everyone looks so happy and relaxed, enjoying life in the sunshine. Young people setting out on life's journey. Who could guess what destiny had in store for them?"

"Loss is part of life," said Charlie. "Sad but true."

"One more thing," said Erika. "I want you both to know John was a good man. The greatest gift he gave you is each other."

– – –

Laura was sitting on the balcony with Charlie back at Orient View. The evening was balmy, and darkness hung over the breadfruit trees in the little garden like a film of dust. In the air was the familiar chorus of the tree frogs.

"You gave Erika some sort of closure tonight, Laura," said Charlie. "We cannot hide from the past."

"True, Charlie, but we need to make sense of it before we can move forward. I realise my search for the past is not always just about me. I have a brother and sister-in-law and soon a nephew or niece. It's unbelievable."

"You'd better believe it!" said Charlie. "We're together now, we have a chance to start over. We can create new memories, ones we can share. You're my sister and I want to get to know you."

Laura stifled a sob.

"Finding you, Charlie, my brother, someone I can call family. It's such a simple thing but for me it is precious – beyond joy." Her voice was trembling. "It's overwhelming for me, Charlie."

Charlie hugged her.

"It's a lot to take in, I know. Emotions are complex things. I will always be here for you but it might help to get away for a while, give yourself some time to process it all," he said.

Tears began to roll down her cheeks.

"You know, Charlie, after my grandmother died, I opened a box of old things that I'd never seen before. They'd been locked away and forgotten. The contents of that box brought me on a journey to a new start – they brought me to Barbados. Do you believe in fate, Charlie?"

"Not really. I like to think we have control of our own lives."

"I came to Barbados pretty much on impulse. I met Erika and I met you – my brother. Don't you think that's strange?"

"Mysterious ways, Laura, mysterious ways."

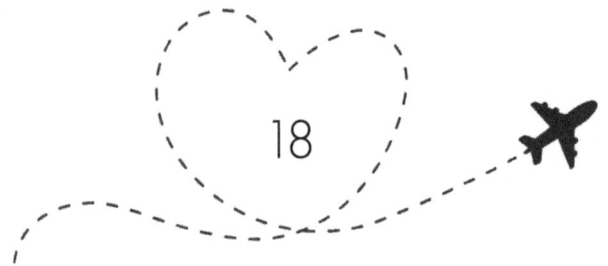

18

"Some beach house," laughed Emma, looking up at the grand porticoed entrance in front of them.

Muffled sounds of music and voices drifted into the air as they approached the open door and entered a large hallway.

It was the night of Blake's party to celebrate the end of the financial year. Laura had promised to go and to invite Emma and Ivan. Tonight, she hoped to have the chance to tell Blake about Charlie – she wanted him to be the first to know – and also to explain that she had to return to Holy Island for a while. She anticipated the evening with mixed feelings. She loved a party but felt far from confident about seeing Blake again.

On arrival they found the parking in front of the house was full. Some cars had lined the road outside, which was where Ivan decided to park. Apparently, this was no soiree for a few friends. They made their way to the back of the house and onto the spectacular terrace, which was arranged with large white sofas and a bar at the far end. The scene was lit by strings of coloured lights; above, a canopy of twinkling stars sparkled in the sky. Beyond the terrace, a rambling garden lit by blue and white icicle lighting hanging in the trees stretched down to a swimming pool. The setting was breathtaking, like entering a fairyland.

A babel of conversation and thumping dance music filled the air. The space was packed with beautiful people in a party mood, dressed in a mind-boggling array of fashion choices, from expensive-looking jeans and brightly coloured shirts to super-short cocktail dresses and long, flowing gowns. Tanned skin dotted with piercings and arms laden with brightly coloured bracelets held glasses of champagne between fingers adorned with jewels. The subtle light flickered on their animated faces as they stood about chattering excitedly.

On seeing them, Blake waved and, working his way through the crowd, came over to welcome them. He was accompanied by a tall blonde woman, the same one Laura had seen him with in Bridgetown months ago. The shock was instant. The pain in her heart was real. Blake kissed her gently on the cheek.

"You look beautiful," he whispered in her ear.

Laura felt herself tense; it felt like a kiss of betrayal. Turning to the blonde, Blake politely introduced them.

"Serena, meet friends of mine, Laura, Emma and Ivan."

Friends. His choice of words stung Laura, especially after what had passed between them. It was the small things, she thought, that showed the feelings, and for

Laura it felt like the final put-down. Serena's cold blue eyes surveyed them, unsmiling and dismissive. She said nothing but put her arm proprietarily through Blake's, her tanned fingers hanging languidly, showing off their pearl nail polish, her wrist weighed down with a stunning selection of gold bangles. Serena gave them a smug look and snuggled closer to Blake, implying they were more than friends. *Okay, Serena, I get it*, thought Laura, *you and Blake are together.*

Serena was wearing a long, white, silk dress with a thin silver belt around her tiny waist. *Ice maiden*, thought Laura, but she looked magnificent and Laura could feel her confidence suddenly take a dive. Serena was obviously part of Blake's circle in New York. Had this woman been in the background the whole time? Laura's first instinct was to walk away, but there were Emma and Ivan to consider. They knew nothing of the change in dynamic between herself and Blake. They had been really looking forward to the party but now everything had changed. Taking several deep breaths, she struggled to keep calm.

Blake looked preoccupied as he led them towards the bar.

"Come and have a drink," he said. "Try one of Serena's cocktails, she made them specially for tonight."

Did she now? thought Laura. "Red wine for me," she said pointedly.

"I'll try one," said Emma, being friendly.

Blake handed Laura a red wine and Emma a cloudy drink with a piece of lime on a cocktail stick across the top.

"A rum special for tonight," he said.

Emma took a sip. "That's delicious, Serena, what's in it?" She was still being friendly.

"It's a secret," replied Serena, her American accent sounding cool and detached. It was the first time she had spoken.

Rude! thought Laura.

"It looks like syrup of figs, so be careful, Emma," she said, surprised at her own uncharacteristic and hardly disguised sarcasm. She wished instantly that she had shown more self-control, but too late now. Emma laughed good-naturedly but Laura caught a shade of displeasure pass over Serena's face. She looked stunned by the unexpected and vitriolic put-down. Giving them all a withering look, Serena left on the pretext of attending to the buffet. As the ice maiden moved away, Laura caught the musky fragrance of expensive perfume and she felt deeply hurt. She knew Serena would be with Blake tonight. Looking up, she thought she saw a flicker of amusement in Blake's eyes, but she didn't care. Her heart was pounding. She downed her wine with defiant zeal, then sipped a second more leisurely, but she was still on edge. A few minutes later, she felt a touch on her shoulder.

"Come and dance, feisty lady." Blake's outstretched hand invited her.

So, thought Laura, *my little outburst didn't go unnoticed.* Forcing a smile and with a calmness she was far from feeling, she put her wine carefully down on the small table in front of her and got up with Blake to dance. The music now was soft and the wine had given her a warm glow.

"I didn't know how things would be between us tonight," he said quietly, watching her face.

A riposte was on the tip of her tongue but she restrained herself.

"Things are fine." Laura's response was cool, her voice unsteady.

They moved slowly to the light reggae beat. The words of the Jason Mraz song "I'm Yours" in the background floated through her mind. Laura had forgotten how powerful music can be in arousing emotions. Feeling sad she drew instinctively closer to Blake, her whole body silently yearning for him.

Serena re-entered the room, eyelashes fluttering, with a young man in tow, and they began dancing close by. As they swayed to the rhythm of the music her long, flowing dress shimmered against her lightly tanned skin, giving her an ethereal quality. She looked radiant and Laura understood how Blake could be so attracted to this woman.

Breathing in Laura's perfumed fragrance Blake was overcome with the memory of how good she felt in his arms and a slow heat stirred in him. He drew Laura closer and kissed her lips gently. Hot tears sprang in Laura's eyes, she blinked them back hard, determined not to let Blake see her cry. She suddenly felt lightheaded.

"I need to sit down," she said feebly.

Leaving Blake, Laura went out to a quiet part of the terrace to be alone and breathe the evening air. Moments later, she heard Blake's voice.

"You okay, Laura?" He had an uncertain look in his

eyes. "Laura, I need to speak with you. This is possibly not a good time, it never is."

Now you want to talk, she thought. Feelings of insecurity engulfed her. Surely, he wasn't going to end things in such a public way.

"I've been doing a lot of thinking, Laura, I've—"

Laura interrupted him. "I'm glad you've worked through some things, Blake, I really am. But I think the truth is you feel entitled to go after whatever you want."

"Seriously, is that how you see this?" Blake was thrown off balance.

"You saw I was vulnerable," she said softly. "And you took advantage."

"You'd be wrong. What is happening here, Laura?"

"I don't think this is going to work between us, Blake."

"You decided that this second?"

"I should have seen it earlier," she said quietly. She just knew it was the wrong time to talk.

"Look, Laura, I leave tomorrow for Toronto. I will be away for at least a week, we need to talk when I return." His voice was earnest.

Laura was no longer listening; her mind was reeling at the news of Blake's imminent departure. As each moment passed it became more difficult to be near to Blake. Just being close to him made her want him more. She wanted to tell him how much she loved him – but she didn't. She felt it wasn't something Blake wanted to hear. Tears threatened once more but she was determined to keep it together. It had been a big mistake to come tonight. Feeling faint, she asked Blake to get her a glass of water. As he left, she looked up and saw Serena watching them from the other end of the terrace. Laura could see her clearly – she had a face like thunder. When Blake returned, Laura suggested he leave her alone. She said it without thinking and she saw him pull back.

Blake had hoped to talk to Laura at least, but it was not the right moment. He could see she was in no mood for conversation. He was overcome with a tight feeling in his chest.

The party intensified as champagne corks popped and laughter filled the air. Couples who had been sitting on the terrace got up and wandered back to the large room to join in the dancing. Revellers passed, carrying bottles of wine and plates of food from the buffet. After a while, Laura glanced around – Blake was nowhere to be seen. She felt saddened that things between herself and Blake had to end this way. Here in Barbados with Blake, she seemed to be at the mercy of her emotions at a time in her life when she most wanted to feel in control. Seeing Ivan twirling Emma on the dance floor, both in high spirits, she felt envious of their loving and apparently uncomplicated closeness. Laura told herself that there had been no suitable opportunity that evening to tell Blake she was returning to Holy Island for a while, but the truth was she had taken the path of least resistance. All night she had been fighting to keep strong and now she had no fight left in her. A dullness had fallen over the party and her eyes clouded with tears. Emma came over to sit with her and remarked on how pale she looked.

"I'm tired," Laura told her, but in truth she was heartbroken.

"Me too," agreed Emma, picking up on her friend's mood. "I'll get Ivan to take us home."

Unable to find Blake, they left the beach house without saying goodbye.

Back at Orient View, Laura's mind was in overdrive. She had entered a territory with Blake that she had vowed to avoid. Was this the same man she had fallen in love with? Who had helped her through so much? She could feel her dreams being swept away. She'd been a fool to get caught up with them in the first place. She tried to think clearly and be rational but it was difficult when her heart was pulling her in a different direction.

A bewildering confusion of feelings whirled around in her head, keeping her from sleeping. She had so many conflicting emotions. The memories of her parents, discovering Charlie was her brother, falling in love with Blake. It was all too much for her to deal with. Laura yearned for peace and solitude – to be alone, to have time to reflect. She was beginning to see only one end in sight. Tomorrow she would speak to Liam and Erika. Instead of signing a new contract, she would return to Holy Island.

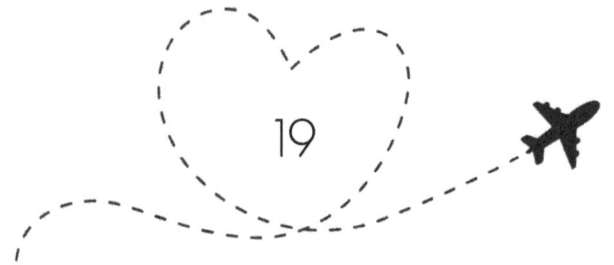

19

It was in a very subdued and downcast frame of mind that Laura paid a farewell visit to Liam and Erika. They had high hopes she would return after the long break, so were understandably very disappointed.

"I was just going over the final monies raised at the school fair before we print the amount in the school magazine. We were well supported by everyone and we raised eight thousand Bajan dollars. Blake generously donated a further twenty thousand from Cargo Air to be used solely for library funding. We have more than enough for a new facility as well as new books for seniors. A special account has been set aside for furniture as well as renovations that need to be made. We're going to have a new lower school library, Laura." Erika was trying to sound upbeat.

"That's wonderful," said Laura quietly.

"I had hoped you'd be here to see it," said Erika.

Laura blinked furiously to fight back the tears.

"I can't tell you," said Erika mournfully, "how sorry we are to lose you, how much we would love you to stay. I know you have a lot to think about but if you should ever change your mind…" Her voice broke away and she moved forward and kissed Laura gently on the cheek.

Feeling uncomfortable, Laura couldn't speak. She turned to leave. Liam stood in the doorway. He seemed unable to think how he could comfort her and instead just stood there helplessly. Brushing away her tears, Laura hugged him tightly and whispered goodbye.

As she walked along the corridor, the joyful sound of children's voices singing wafted from the hall. The familiar chimes of the bell rang out, marking the end of the school day. She realised this was the last time she would hear these comforting sounds. Entering her classroom, Laura simply picked up her bag and a few books and the world of St. Catherine's closed behind her.

The last eight months had been a time of personal growth for Laura. She had arrived grieving and full of questions. Barbados had given her both solace and joy during the emotional rollercoaster that had become her life since the death of her grandmother. She loved the island; it had started to feel like home. This beautiful tropical island had given her so much, but now it was time to leave.

The last few days on Barbados flew by with cruel speed. Laura said her goodbyes and her heart couldn't face anymore – she begged to be left alone. Blake was still in Toronto on business, and she was thankful she didn't have to face him.

The hour of departure arrived and Emma, Ivan and Sean insisted on being there.

"If only things had been different," Emma said sadly. "But there's no point in going there. I promise to come and see you on Holy Island."

Aylen came running from the beach. She flung her arms around Laura, hugging her silently. Then, leaning back, she spoke in her inimitable Bajan way.

"Don't rush de brush and trow way de paint."

Laura gave a weak smile to show she understood what Aylen meant: don't make hasty decisions you could regret. *Too late for that*, she thought.

A car horn tooted in the courtyard. The moment to leave had come and Laura began to crumble inside. Charlie got out and waved hello. Ivan and Sean collected her cases and put them in the boot. They hugged her one last time. Charlie put his arm around her. As she entered the courtyard, the smell of the jasmine and magnolia hit her. It would always be the smell of Barbados for her. Laura got into the car and through a blur of tears bid a silent adieu to Bay Street.

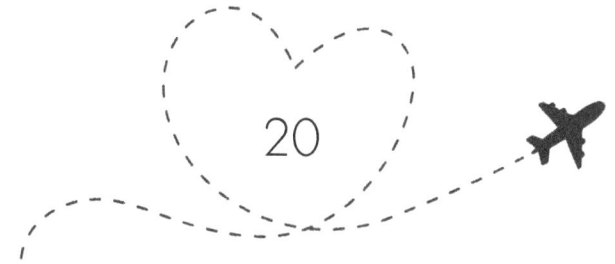

20

Since returning to Holy Island, Laura had had a great deal of time for reflection as she spent night after night alone in the cottage she had grown up in, staring with vacant eyes into the empty fireplace, listening to the ticking of the old clock on the mantelpiece. The calm serenity of the island soothed her at first. She'd imagined that she would feel at home, but she didn't. Outwardly, she had changed very little, but inwardly she scarcely recognised the person she'd been when she left. Around her the stone cottages, once so warm and familiar, now appeared to be cold and lifeless. She missed everything about Barbados. The apartment on Bay Street where she'd spent long, sunlit days filled with warmth and laughter and friends, had been the happiest times she had ever known. Her beloved Holy Island could give her no comfort.

Hoping the fresh, cool air would help to clear her mind, Laura took a walk to the beach, which was deserted except for a few gulls. Only their constant shrill and the steady pulsing of the waves broke the silence. As she walked, she noticed that empty shell cases from the North Sea crabs were caught among the seaweed at the water's edge. Several pieces of blue and turquoise antique glass caught her eye as they glittered in the wet sand. She picked them up and slipped them into her pocket, as she had done many times before. Leaving the sand, she reached the dunes. The tall grass on the hill seemed to whisper sweetly in the breeze. Around her, the yellow and white flowers of the eyebright glittered with dew. Laura stood and stared into the horizon, watching the mist curl and rise over the sea. She recalled with poignant clarity the pure heaven of making love with Blake on the beach in Barbados. A special memory she could hang on to when the rest had faded. Blake had seemed to care, but she had read the whole thing wrong. When she had tried to get closer he had pulled away. It was time to put it behind her and focus on the future.

David spent most of his time now in Glasgow on a course in anaesthetics. He was preoccupied with work. The day he drove her home from Edinburgh airport on her return, he seemed not to notice her pallor. Even if he had, he would never have guessed the truth. Unable to take much time away from the hospital, David had suggested that she come up to Glasgow. Laura wanted time with David; she wanted to catch up. They hadn't spoken much since she'd been away. The more she thought about it, the more the idea of going to Glasgow made sense.

Early afternoon the next day, Laura made the two-hour train journey from Berwick to Glasgow. David met her at the station. He greeted her warmly before driving them the short distance to his apartment in Glasgow's West End.

"Here we are," he said, bringing the car to a halt outside a blond sandstone building. "Crown Gardens," he grinned, taking a set of keys from his jacket pocket.

Stepping out of the car, Laura glanced up at the four-storey tenement block in front of her its characteristic rows of bay windows facing like eyes onto the street below. She loved these magnificent homes, erected in Victorian times to house an influx of workers into the city. They now epitomised the very character of Glasgow. David led the way up several stone steps to a large black front door that, when opened, revealed a rectangular close with wonderful period features. To one side, a stairway with wrought-iron balustrades wound its way upwards alongside walls decorated to dado level with pale green ceramic tiles. As Laura breathed in the musty smell, her mind immediately transported back in time to the old flat she had shared with fellow students in Edinburgh. It seemed like a lifetime ago.

"I'm on the second floor, Laura. There's no lift, I'm afraid," he said.

On reaching a landing, David unlocked another door and they entered his apartment.

"I'm close to the hospital and well placed for road links back to Holy Island. It's a useful place to be."

Laura followed him into a fairly modern kitchen. The old black-and-white floor tiles delighted her and added to the charm of the place. Glancing through the window, she took in the views over an unkempt communal garden at the back.

"It's lovely, David," she said.

David dropped his keys on the kitchen table, and taking off his jacket, hung it across the back of a chair. Turning to the coffee machine, he picked up a jug and started to fill it.

"Have a look around, Laura, I'll make coffee."

There was an uneasiness between them and Laura was glad of the opportunity to leave him to it. She was finding it more than a little tense being in David's company again and she had no doubt he must have been feeling the same.

The place seemed pleasant enough. The bathroom was modern. Both bedrooms were a good size but only contained a bed, drawers and wardrobe. David's clothing could be seen in one of them, where the door was slightly ajar, and on the wall she glimpsed the shell collage that she had given him years ago. Somehow it looked out of place in a city flat. Laura left her small luggage bag in the second bedroom next door. The bay-windowed lounge was also quite sparsely furnished, with two dark grey sofas and a table and chairs. In one corner an untidy bookcase disgorged medical books and journals. There was not a plant or living thing in sight. The apartment revealed very little of personal interest; it was drab and in need of colour. Laura began to feel very sad for David... until she saw something unexpected, a large oil painting on canvas. It hung unframed on the white wall above the Victorian fireplace. Lindisfarne Castle at dawn, looking resplendent high above the silvery, mercurial waters of the North Sea. The morning sky was ablaze with the red and gold fire of a rising sun shining brightly through the grey clouds, giving the scene a mystical feel. It was the only decoration in the flat. A little spark of passion, thought Laura, in an otherwise dreary home. Laura stood and studied it. Memories are strange things, she mused. They can lie dormant for years then out of nowhere something simple can bring them flooding back. She pictured herself walking with friends to the castle, which to a small child had seemed to loom large above her, dark and rather sinister. As they pushed their way among the tangled grass, which nearly reached to her waist, she felt very adventurous. They sat in the walled garden alongside, enjoying a picnic of iced buns from the local bakery and drinking lemonade. As the sun began to set they walked home together. David was there – he always made her feel safe. When she looked back years later she realised that, thanks to David's friendship, she came through a lot better. Laura loved him for that.

"Wow," she said. "David, I love your painting."

"Thanks," he replied, coming through with two coffees, which he put down on the table. "It's my dream to return to Holy Island to live one day."

"We were so lucky to grow up there," said Laura.

"Ah, those enchanting days." David gazed nostalgically at the picture.

"Ken Lilburn, the old fisherman, painted it. He was quite the artist but would never sell his work." David paused, his eyes still on the canvas. "I used to chat to him sometimes as he painted in his boat-shed. Beth gave it to me when her dad passed away."

"He's managed to capture the magic of our island, hasn't he?" said Laura wistfully.

"That's what I love about it." David looked at her, his expression softening. His eyes lingered a little too long for Laura's comfort and she turned away to pick up her coffee. David sighed. He looked embarrassed and transferred his gaze to the window.

"Anyway," he said, "there are several restaurants nearby we could go to but I thought I'd cook tuna pasta tonight – your favourite. Give us time to catch up."

"Sounds lovely, thank you," she said, smiling up into his face.

Laura guessed David was trying his best to make her feel relaxed but she knew they were far from comfortable with each other. The quick glances, the awkward pauses – the tension in the air was palpable.

Over dinner, David opened up about his work at the infirmary, which Laura found interesting. He was on safe ground now and the strain between them began to ease. David turned towards her.

"I've been thinking back to the old days, our time in Edinburgh." Laura wondered where he was going with this.

"The friends I had haven't met up for months, a year even. Some have moved away, one has married, another has gone to Manchester. They seem to have dropped out of sight."

Laura could sense his loneliness and it tugged at her heart.

"Lives change, David, people move on, it's inevitable," she said gently. "New friends come along in time."

"It's been lonely here," he said. "I've missed you."

Laura remained silent. Putting her hand to her brow,

she sighed, troubled by his comments. She still carried guilt. She cared for David, they had grown up together, been good friends, nothing could take that away. David mistakenly read her new, soft mood, and he leaned towards her as if he intended to kiss her. Looking into his eyes for a split-second, Laura felt a glimmer of something long forgotten, but she pulled away. The last thing she wanted was this kind of complication. There followed an embarrassing pause, with each considering what had just happened. David leant back, shaking his head and forcing a smile. He was doing his best to hide his hurt feelings. Laura inhaled and bit her lip. She regretted being so obvious, but David had taken her by surprise.

"I'm sorry," she said.

David was watching her intently; he was about to say something. Laura waited.

"Why did you have to go to Barbados?" he asked.

And there it was! The question he'd been wanting to ask all night. Laura heaved a sigh; she didn't want to fall out with him.

"You know why, David," she replied calmly.

The resolve of her answer only served to make him more persistent.

"I've spent a lot of time by myself. I've had time to think." He hesitated to look at Laura for a moment. "I love you, Laura."

David looked searchingly at her. His grey eyes looked weary and hopeful at the same time. He seemed vulnerable. Laura couldn't bear to hurt him, but she felt this curious numbness.

"I still want to marry you," he whispered.

Laura heard the pleading in his voice and saw the kindness in his eyes. Minutes ago her answer would have been, "David, I can't marry you, I'm in love with someone else." These were the words she should have said, but they stuck in her throat. She watched him as he spoke. David too had a way with him, a look in his eye. Her love for Blake felt like a foolish dream. David was offering her his love. He was a caring, stable man – that counted for something. They had a foundation of friendship. She looked at him anxiously.

"Do you think we could be happy, David," she asked, "knowing I have uncertainties?"

"Without a doubt," he replied.

"Give me a little more time, David," she said gently.

When she'd decided to come to Glasgow Laura, perhaps naively, hadn't expected a situation like this. Leaving Holy Island to go to Barbados had changed her, changed her life. Deep down she'd hoped David had moved on, too: new city, new colleagues, a girlfriend, even. Apparently not! His feelings were unambiguous. David wanted to cling to what used to be but she had moved on. Laura wanted to change the subject, try to lighten the mood, but that seemed unlikely now. The atmosphere of the evening had become strained once more, the conversation stunted. In her mind, she and David had always been just friends; real life, however, was much more complicated. Tonight, Laura wanted to protect him from an outright rebuff. Now she wasn't sure what the outcome would be. Tears welled in her eyes.

"Is anything wrong, Laura?" David asked.

"No, not at all." Her voice was muffled as she fought to keep it steady.

"You're sure?" David was watching her.

Laura forced herself to look up at him and smile and answer lightly, "Quite sure."

"Thank heaven," he said. "For a moment there I thought you were crying."

The next morning the weather in Glasgow was cooler, the day a little greyer. It was drizzling outside. Finding it impossible to sleep, Laura had risen early and made coffee. She knew David hadn't slept well – she'd heard him tossing and turning restlessly in the bedroom next door. Laura sat quietly in the lounge. In the grey dusk of an autumn morning she noticed the leaves on the trees had started to change. Russet reds and golden browns brought colour to the street. David came through to join her.

"Did you sleep well, Laura?"

"I did, thank you." There was no point in saying otherwise.

"I had hoped you'd stay longer, I wanted more time with you."

"I need to get back, David. There are things to sort out."

"Perhaps next time," he smiled.

Laura felt wretched. Would there be a next time? Standing up, she hugged him affectionately. Outside, it had stopped raining. Minutes later, they left Crown Gardens together and headed into town. David would drop her at the station. For Laura, it had been a confusing and somewhat depressing visit. Explaining her feelings to David, let alone trying to understand them herself, was proving much harder to do than she had ever imagined.

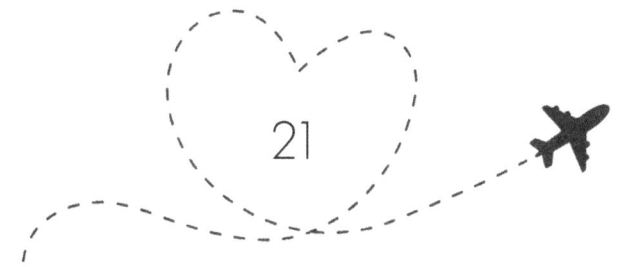

21

Blake was relaxing in his Toronto hotel suite, watching C.B.S news. His thoughts were on the impending meeting in thirty minutes. After days of intense negotiations, he was close to an agreement with the Canadian company. He sat back to enjoy a morning cup of coffee when his phone rang. It was his mother. This was an unusual event in itself, but when he heard her speak it rang alarm bells.

"It's me, Blake." Her voice sounded weak. He could hear gentle weeping on the other end.

"Your father's had a heart attack, Blake. It's serious."

"I'm in Toronto, Mom. It's okay. I can be there in a few hours."

"He's in Presbyterian East 68th. Please come as soon as you can." The phone went dead.

Blake turned off the TV and sat brooding for a moment, drinking his coffee. But he couldn't concentrate for thinking about what was going on in New York. *To hell with it,* he thought, *I'm leaving now.* A few phone calls later he'd cancelled the talks, left a message for Kristina and arranged a private jet from Pearson Airport to New York.

Several hours later, a taxi dropped him outside the Presbyterian. Navigating his way through the massive hospital buildings, he found the cardiology department. He was shocked when he saw his mother; her face was tear-stained, her eyes red and sore. Her legs were unsteady as he walked her through to a nearby waiting room. They sat together, Blake holding her tight. A long moment passed before she began to speak.

"They've discovered major heart disease. Your father needs a quadruple bypass. If anything happens to him, Blake..." She left the sentence unfinished as a doctor approached them.

He spoke calmly, in a serious tone. "Mrs Degas, your husband is still in surgery. Later, he will be moved to critical care to be monitored. I'm afraid he will be unconscious for hours but tomorrow he will be allowed visitors. He's in good hands. I suggest you go home and try to get some rest."

In the taxi, Rhonda couldn't stop crying. The full extent of the ordeal was becoming apparent to Blake.

"It's been horrific, Blake," she said. "Your father works ninety-hour weeks. He is obsessed with the company, with the next project. He sleeps badly – gets up early – eats poorly. Is it any wonder his body has given up?" she said, wiping her eyes.

Blake was incredulous. "What kind of life have you been living?"

Rhonda tried to avoid looking directly at him. When she did, he saw great sadness in her eyes.

"Separate lives," she admitted at length. "I feel I don't know him anymore."

"Why didn't you tell me?"

"Because your father can see nothing wrong. I've been hiding so much for so long. I feel nervous all the time."

Blake sensed her helplessness; he saw it flash across her face.

"That's what secrets do to you," he said. "You can't go on living like this."

"He will never change, Blake."

"I don't think he has much choice, Mom. He will come to accept what has happened," Blake said, taking her hand.

"You've got many good years to look forward to, try to concentrate on that."

"I hope so," Rhonda smiled gently but without any mirth.

"It must have been hell, but you've survived," he said.

Rhonda remained silent but they were both thinking the same thing: how had it come to this? Blake put his arms around her.

"First thing tomorrow we'll go to the hospital," he said. Rhonda nodded.

Weary with anxiety, she said goodnight and went to bed. Although it was only six p.m. she fell into an exhausted sleep. Blake slouched back in the armchair, turning the day's events over in his mind. He realised his parents had an uphill struggle in front of them to rebuild their lives in a new direction. It dawned on him how much he loved them. He'd been trying to break away from them for so long he'd lost sight of that fact. He didn't have to share their values and beliefs, but he would be there to support them. *Life is a journey*, he reflected, *we can all grow and learn.*

As if on cue, his phone rang.

"It's Kristina, Blake."

"Are you okay?" he asked.

"Yes – yes…" Her voice trailed away. "I want to come to New York, but I'm afraid."

"What are you trying to tell me, Kristina?"

"Sorry, Blake, it's not a good time."

"I'll come and get you tomorrow," he said firmly.

She put the phone down. Blake tried to call her back but there was no answer. He knew this would not have happened six months ago, Kristina reaching out to him. The tone of her voice worried him; he began to think the worst. After the hospital tomorrow, he would drive up to East Hampton.

Early afternoon the next day, Blake was parking on the drive outside Kristina and Steve Trent's home in East Hampton. The boughs on the trees were creaking and the leaves shaking in the afternoon breeze as he rang the doorbell. It was Kristina who answered the door – Trent wasn't at home. *Good*, thought Blake, *makes a change*. He was appalled to see how thin she looked. Her face was pale and her eyes hollow. On seeing Blake, she threw herself into his arms, sobbing with relief. It didn't take long for Blake to realise that Kristina was in a bad way.

"Where's Steve?" he asked.

"He won't be home till later," she said tearfully.

"If you want to come with me, go and get your things." Blake spoke quietly.

Kristina hesitated for a moment; she took a small step.

"Steve will be furious if I leave," she said.

"The choice is yours, Kristina, do you want to come with me?"

"Yes, but I don't know what he'll do. I'm scared."

"Nothing," said Blake. "He's a coward. I'm here to support you. Could this be the moment to leave him and move on?"

"I hope so," she sighed.

"Well, go and get your things."

There was no time for further discussion. Kristina went upstairs. Just then, Trent's car drew up in the drive. He looked questioningly at the parked car and stopped to look inside the windows. As he opened the front door, Kristina was coming downstairs with her suitcase.

"What's going on?" he said heatedly.

"I told you, Steve, my father's had a heart attack. I'm going to see him."

"You're going nowhere, lady," he said coldly.

"Please, Steve, I want to go," she pleaded.

Blake now came through to the hall. He saw Kristina start to tremble.

"She's coming with me," said Blake calmly.

Kristina held her breath. Ignoring her, Trent addressed Blake.

"Get out," he shouted. "She's my wife, she's going nowhere."

Kristina stood cowering on the stairs; she was biting the inside of her lip. She looked at Trent, fear in her eyes. Blake placed himself between them.

"I'm not leaving without her. Kristina, put your case in the car," Blake said evenly.

Kristina began weeping. Blake didn't move. Trent gritted his teeth and moved towards him; with his arm in the air, he made a lunge at Blake. It wasn't clear what happened next, but one moment Trent was standing, the next he slid down the wall of the hallway. Blake ushered Kristina out of the front door. Trent looked dazed – he was attempting to pick himself up as Blake began to speak.

"It would be better to keep this simple," said Blake. "There's bound to be unpleasant publicity, it's the sort of thing the press love." He paused dramatically. "You could lose your licence to practice law. You'd be finished."

Trent cleared his throat. Blake could see him almost shrink under the effect of his words.

"Perhaps you should give some thought to how you've made Kristina suffer – keep away from her."

Blake left the house and closed the door.

Kristina was still shaking.

"He'll come after me," she said, tears running down her cheeks.

"Not if he knows what's good for him," said Blake, gently squeezing her hand.

"Thank you, Blake," she whispered.

As they drove away, the street was the epitome of calm, belying the drama that had just been enacted inside the house. For Blake, the last 24 hours had seemed surreal.

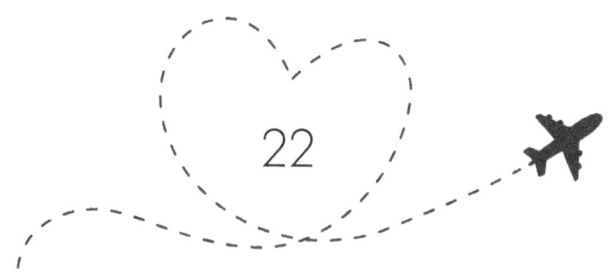

22

Unexpectedly, David returned to Holy Island on Friday evening, having left Glasgow after his shift at the hospital. He managed to catch the causeway. Even though it was after ten p.m., Laura met up with him and they walked to their local for a drink. The full moon was rising high in the heavens and the air was crisp. Tonight was lock-in at the pub. No police on the island, stay as long as you like, no closing time until the landlord says so. Holy Island was pleasantly cut off from the outside world. The panelled room was cosy, lit by a glowing fire; it was warm and comfortable after the cold of outside. They sat in their usual corner and Eddie the barman waved over to her in welcome as David got the drinks. For Laura, it felt like old times.

"I feel we need to clear the air." David jumped in as he sat down beside her. "We haven't talked about marriage for a while," he said.

Laura raised her head and gave David a steady look. It

was a conversation she had hoped not to have again with him so soon.

"I can offer you security, Laura."

"Spoken like a true romantic," she teased.

"I think it's essential to a happy marriage," he replied defensively. "I do love you, Laura," he said seriously.

"Do you, David?" she asked gently.

"Of course, I thought it was obvious. Why else would I ask you to marry me?"

There was silence for a moment. Laura felt a mix of emotions hit her all at once. The great affection she had for David and sadness that he seemed unable to move on. Part of her wanted to end this embarrassing situation here and now. She looked anxiously at him, her blue eyes enormous in her pale face.

"I feel the need to explain something," she began.

"No, you don't need to. I understand."

Laura had been steeling herself to tell it all, to unburden, because it was all becoming too much for her. But, looking around the room, she hadn't the courage. She wished they had gone somewhere more private. The pub, with so many people around, was not the place to start such a serious and frank discussion. Neither did she want to spoil his first evening home. She would wait until tomorrow. She clutched her gin and tonic.

"I don't know what to say, David, can we discuss this when we're alone?"

"Well, yes, of course," he replied. His voice sounded somewhat surprised, and he looked at her reproachfully. Laura smiled then skilfully changed the subject.

"Tell me, David, how's the course going?" This worked out well because all she had to do was sit back and listen.

Thankfully, they didn't stay too long because David was tired. He walked her home and kissed her gently on the cheek. He wanted to linger, but Laura drew away from him.

"It's late, David, I'll see you tomorrow." So saying, she hurried out of the wintery night into the cottage.

Lying in bed in the darkness, Laura replayed the evening's conversation with David in her head. Her grandmother always considered friendship the way to lasting happiness in a marriage. Laura didn't believe it. There was no mistaking the difference between what she felt for David and the feelings Blake aroused in her. There was no rationale to it, no logic. Laura craved that indefinable excitement of being in love. The dazzling high, the joy, the passion that made her feel so alive, made her see life with an intensity like never before. She had that with Blake. David, for all his worthy qualities, would never be able to give her that. They both deserved better. Even if it risked their friendship, Laura knew she must be honest with David, but she had never been so reluctant to do something in her whole life. Turning over in bed, she pulled the duvet over her shoulders, feeling cold and sick at heart. She wanted to sleep and forget everything.

The next day she met up with David and they took a walk along the dirt track towards the castle. Laura had a strong sense of foreboding at the thought of seeing him again, making her feel very nervous. David, too, seemed to be introspective today. Feeling wretched and finding it difficult to speak, Laura sat down on the turf and put her hands in her coat pockets. She looked forlornly at David, who was now seated next to her. Never good at communicating her feelings, she didn't know where to start. David's expression was sombre. He watched as the anxious uncertainty crossed Laura's face. They sat for a moment or two, which seemed much longer to Laura. Eventually it was David who spoke first.

"You've changed, haven't you, Laura? Towards me, I mean." He looked questioningly at her.

"I suppose I have," she replied, avoiding his gaze.

"Your voice is different, you're different. It's no use pretending, is it?" he said quietly.

Their eyes met and held. Laura turned away, a lump in her throat.

"We used to talk about everything," he said. "Remember those days? I thought they would have been ours forever."

"I'm sorry, David."

"I've been doing a lot of thinking," he continued. "I realise you've hardly mentioned Barbados since your return. I thought you would have so much to tell me."

It was the first time Laura had heard David talk this way. Of course, he was right, she hadn't told him much about Barbados. She wouldn't know where to begin. Then again, he hadn't asked either and she wondered if he was really interested. Nevertheless, he sounded deflated. She knew he was trying to reach her.

"It was always in my mind that we would marry one day," he said softly. "I would look after you."

"I'm a grown woman, David, I can take care of myself."

Today, David also seemed different. Laura noticed a definite shift in his attitude. He was no longer taking her for granted. Looking at him in the soft glow of the afternoon light, she thought how attractive he was. His eyes, especially, were kind. Yet it was as though she hardly knew him at all.

David lifted his shoulders despondently. "Your thoughts are far away these days, I can't seem to get through to you."

"I feel… I feel…" Laura searched for words. "I feel empty," she said flatly.

David didn't answer, but put his arm around her, and the comfort eased the stress momentarily.

"Please, David, don't feel sorry for me." Her voice was hoarse.

David turned away from her, unsure, and it touched Laura's heart.

"We used to be so happy together – I love you, Laura."

"I love you, too, David, and I will always want you in my life, but I'm not in love with you."

"Love, in love – they're the same thing," he said assuredly.

Laura understood. She had thought that way once, but not anymore.

"They really aren't, David," she said gently. "I'm sorry."

"Is that all you have to say?" He sounded exasperated. She knew he was hurting.

"It's all I've got," she whispered.

Laura felt a pang of compassion. Things between herself and David had changed forever. In that moment of desolation, she realised that their friendship would never be the same. David hugged Laura tightly. Looking up at the sky, he spoke dispiritedly.

"The clouds are gathering. I think we should go."

There was nothing more to be said. The next day, David left Holy Island and returned to Glasgow.

Being honest with David had saddened her, but she had to be true to herself. As the days went by she tried to wrench her mind from dwelling on Blake, but without success. The ache was all inside, deep and dull; she felt it would never go away. Laura wondered how Blake had been since she had left. She guessed his ego may have taken a dent but thought that he'd probably already moved on. These thoughts were perpetually on her mind and made her restless. Each day she tried to fill the emptiness, each day she failed. She had known loss and loneliness in her life and had always found ways to cope. She knew she would do so again, but perhaps not here on Holy Island. *Tomorrow is a new day,* she told herself. It was time to turn the page, start a new chapter in her life.

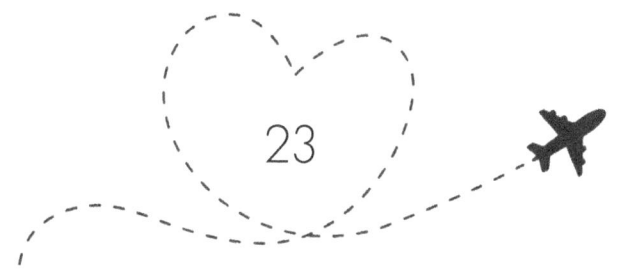

23

Blake had chosen to reserve a table by the window at a restaurant on the fifth floor of a hotel near Central Park. Outside, he could see New York beautifully lit up in a colourful aura emanating from the city lights. He hoped it was the perfect place to have a difficult but long-overdue conversation with Serena. It offered just enough privacy but, on the other hand, was public enough so as to discourage her from making a scene.

So far tonight, Blake had said very little. Throughout the meal Serena had still been miffed about the way she felt Blake had treated her at the beach house party.

"I don't know what got into you, making a fool of yourself with that girl," she hissed between mouthfuls of pasta.

"Her name is Laura, you know that very well. I introduced you."

Blake paused, reigning in his irritation. If at all possible, he wanted to get this evening over with in a civilised way.

"Why did you invite her in the first place?" Serena couldn't let it go.

"Serena, you don't have the right to say who I can invite to my home."

"For goodness' sake, we were practically engaged."

Pure fantasy, Blake thought, but left it.

"Your family love me. I get on brilliantly with them."

It was the final shot in her arsenal. At one time, it was true; his mother would have been delighted to see him married to Serena. She was someone from their circle. Now, Rhonda was overwhelmed with worry about his father lying in the hospital, of which Serena knew nothing and he intended to keep it that way.

"The point is…" Blake began, but Serena interrupted him.

"The point is," she said aggressively, "I'm not happy at all with you being so obvious. Then flying off the next day. It reflects on me, you know." She took a sip of her wine.

Blake could hardly believe his ears; she was wholly concerned with herself.

"Are you jealous, Serena?" he asked testily.

"Of what?" she scoffed, banging her glass down on the table.

"Serena, I've asked you to meet me here tonight because we need to have an honest talk." Blake's voice was urgent, insistent.

Serena flashed him a quick smirk.

"Come on, then," she sighed impatiently. She watched him across the table as he spoke, shifting in her seat and fiddling with the wine glasses in front of her.

"We've had fun together, Serena, but it doesn't feel right anymore." He was trying to be diplomatic.

At first Serena, thought he was joking, but after a while she began to realise he was being serious.

"Let's not talk about this now. How about we go out? Imagine what fun it would be to stay out all night then go back to mine." Leaning in closer, she stretched her arms across the table and took his hands in hers. She was eyeing him, a steady, unashamedly sexual come-on.

"I can give you whatever you want," she said enticingly.

The thought sickened him. Blake could smell her – the musky perfume she always wore. He looked at her. She was like a beautiful statue, no smile, not a trace of warmth in her eyes. He was finding her unpleasant to be around. Tension was rising in him by the minute. It was becoming crystal clear that he was going to have to spell it out.

"I don't want you to come to the beach house again," he said, more sharply than he meant to, letting go of her hands. Serena sat upright in her chair; she looked as though she had swallowed a stone.

"I know you'll be okay, Serena; we have to—" but Serena cut him short.

"Excuse me," she said, turning on him. "You jerk," she sneered. "Who do you think you are? I'm going to meet friends at a bar." Moving her seat back, she picked up her handbag, stood up and flounced out of the room, flicking her long, blonde hair as she went. Blake inhaled deeply, and the tension in his chest began to ease. *One thing less to fret about*, he thought.

Leaving the restaurant, Blake took a yellow cab to the

Harvard club, one of the most exclusive in New York. He didn't go there to mingle with other members; he liked it for its calm, unchanging ambience. He wanted to sit quietly to clear his mind of the clutter of impressions left by the turmoil of recent days. A chance to reflect. As he entered, he looked around and noticed with some satisfaction that the place was just as he hoped – almost empty. Moving through the warm, pleasant rooms, he found a quiet seat in the corner of the bar and ordered a beer.

Thoughts of Laura filled his mind, and feelings of regret engulfed him as he recalled their interaction at the party. Lately, when he was with her, he was overcome with an unfamiliar feeling. It made him want to say things he'd never normally say. What was wrong with him? Usually, he preferred his female companions with no strings attached. He'd met other women, but their attraction seemed superficial, his relationships with them shallow. In one sense, he could have anybody he wanted, but he wanted someone for whom he felt something special. He had liked Laura right from the start, the first time he set eyes on her at the airport. Laura had it all: natural beauty and charm and that extra something that he couldn't put his finger on, which made everything so complete. It was a quality of feeling she brought. When he was with her, she created the most loving and intimate atmosphere. One he'd never experienced before.

The next morning, Blake accompanied his mother and Kristina to the Presbyterian. His father looked frail and lost in the hospital bed. He was wired up to all sorts of monitors that blinked and pulsed, and oxygen to help him breathe. He smiled weakly, seeming pleased to see them. Rhonda fussed over him, gently plumping the pillows and touching his hands lovingly. It struck Blake that it was the first time in years that his family had gathered together, so fractured had the bonds between them become. He felt it strangely befitting somehow that their reunion was taking place in a hospital ward.

After a while, Blake hugged his mother and took Kristina to one side.

"Are you going to be okay?" he asked gently.

"I think so. I feel as though I've been walking through fog, but things are getting clearer."

"You're safe now, Kristina. Remember that!"

"I know, and Mom and Dad need me. We can help each other," she whispered.

He hugged her tightly. Stepping outside, he closed the door behind him. He made his way through the cardiology department, stopping at the nurses' station to thank them. Outside on the street, he took a cab to JFK, anxious to get home to Barbados.

24

Much to Laura's relief, the probate on her grandmother's estate was now completed. The lawyers sent her the appropriate documentation, which meant she could now start the process of selling up. The cottage was built with a garden at the back, the front going onto the cobbled street. The little garden was filled with bushes of white roses, her grandmother's favourite. Laura took a few moments to appreciate being out there on the old wooden bench where her grandmother often sat reading in her later years. The cottage had been a family home for several generations and, on one level, the thought of letting it go was heart-wrenching. The last few weeks felt like an unravelling to Laura. All the ways she had defined her life had changed. If she wanted to move forward and make a fresh start somewhere new, it was necessary to sell. So she remained resolute. Estate agents from Berwick advised her that property on Holy Island was highly sought-after. The island offered a haven for families wishing to relocate for a better quality of life, more so because it had an excellent school. There were also second homeowners looking for a retreat from the urban rat race, somewhere they could eventually retire. The agents expected a swift sale. The following days were spent lovingly packing those things she would need to put into storage for a while. The task brought many memories flooding back, but there was no one to share them with, which made her feel even more alone.

– – –

Laura was finding it almost impossible to be so unhappy and not tell anyone. True to her word, Emma was coming to stay with her for a few days on her trip back to the UK. This gave Laura something practical to focus on. It took her most of the day to sort out the spare room; there was so much nostalgia imbued in each object. However, the simple task of sorting through the chaos had soothed her and she felt more cheerful. The room received a fresh coat of soft white paint, fresh linen on the bed and, as a final gesture to brighten the space, Laura added a blue throw and a few pieces of antique sea glass in a dish by the bedside lamp. The vase Sean had made for her was lovingly placed on the window ledge. Eventually, the space was habitable. Laura stood back after her hard work and surveyed the room, which was now cosy and inviting, ready for her friend. If only life was as easy to fix, she thought.

Emma arrived and was as lively and cheerful as ever. They hugged in welcome, delighted to see each other again. It was autumn and the island was now relatively empty after the hordes of summer visitors. Laura planned to give Emma a whirlwind tour and, for a while, her spirits lifted.

The next day, after a breakfast of fresh poached eggs on toast, they made a start. The air was fresh and the morning bright. Emma was eager to see Lindisfarne Castle. As they passed along the little harbour, it wasn't long before it came into view and didn't disappoint.

"It's fabulous," said Emma. "There's no way better word to describe it, the setting is so iconic."

Reaching the top of the winding path, they stopped to admire the view out to sea.

"Oh, look, there are seals on the rocks below," said Emma excitedly.

"Yes, in autumn the females come ashore to pup," Laura told her.

"Can we get down to that beach over there?" asked Emma, pointing in the distance, where grey seals could be seen bobbing up and down playfully in the water.

"Of course, you can't leave without seeing it."

As they neared the sands, there was a soft moaning sound being carried on the breeze. Emma realised it was coming from the seals.

"They're singing," laughed Laura.

Above them, the noise from the circling gulls got louder. Their strident squawking filled the air. Beneath them, miles of golden sand spread into the distance.

"What a stunning place Holy Island is," gushed Emma. "The epic sky, the crashing waves. It's so romantic."

"Believe it or not, Emma, it is from this very beach that the Vikings first invaded Britain in 793 A.D."

Emma linked her arm through Laura's. Her eyes scanned along the beach as if searching for any marauding Viking stragglers.

"Wow," she said. "You learn something new every day."

That night in the cottage they drank Lindisfarne Mead and ate fresh crab sandwiches, reminiscing about their time together at St. Catherine's, laughing at the antics they'd shared with Ivan and Sean. Neither mentioned the elephant in the room. Neither mentioned Blake.

The following day, they climbed the dunes on the western tip of the island, walking between abundant willow and marram grasses and helleborine orchids still in bloom.

"Holy Island is famous for its orchids and bird life. Soon the light-bellied geese and curlews will arrive to feed on the winter's food from the flats," said Laura.

"It's like being in a wildlife documentary. You're so lucky to have grown up here," laughed Emma.

"It can get very lonely." Laura's words were muted. She was trying not to burden Emma with her unhappiness. Though Emma sensed the melancholy in her friend, she said nothing.

They continued their leisurely walk back towards the priory. As they approached the entrance, a small flock of birds flew from the darkness of the ancient stone walls, giving them both a fright and shaking the dust of centuries down onto them, causing Emma to catch her breath.

"I think I've just been initiated or something," she laughed, wiping her shoulders and shaking her hair.

On entering the vast rectangular hall of the ruin, they saw that soft tints of afternoon sun were creeping over the roofless space. The light was subdued, the ambience peaceful. The long, arched windows open to the elements cast shadows onto the green mossy ground around them. Emma was transfixed.

"It's a bit spooky," she whispered. "It feels like time has stood still on Holy Island."

That night, after dinner in the cottage, Laura opened a bottle of wine. The mood was reflective. Emma was leaving tomorrow, but tonight she was preoccupied.

"I'd never heard of Holy Island till I met you, Laura. Now I'm so taken by its beauty and landscape."

"When I first returned home, I loved the peace and remoteness. It was just what I needed to get away from it all for a while," said Laura.

"It couldn't be more different to Barbados, that's for sure," smiled Emma.

"After a while, I realised how much I had changed. Even my clothes felt wrong. There's not much call for cerise kaftans and swinging earrings here any day of the week, even a hot one. I had to search out my old tops and dark trousers," sighed Laura.

"I noticed," smiled Emma.

"Yes, I'm back among the knitted people, all woolly jumpers and beanies." said Laura, taking a sip of wine. Emma smiled sympathetically, sensing the gloom behind her words. She decided it was the right moment to broach the subject that had been on her mind all along.

"I ran into Blake in Bridgetown just before I left." She

looked at Laura expectantly, waiting for a reply. None was forthcoming, so she persisted.

"He'd been in New York; his father had a heart attack."

Laura was shocked but she tried to remain calm. "I'm sorry to hear that." She meant it sincerely.

Emma was still watching her carefully, determined to get more of a reaction.

"Now he spends his time between New York and Barbados."

Emma's words brought a chill to Laura's heart. The only thing worse than loving someone who was lost to you was thinking of them with someone else. Laura felt nauseous.

"Blake will be with Serena," she said softly.

Emma seemed surprised. "Apparently Serena hasn't been in Barbados since the fateful party. She and Blake split some time before. They are not together, although not for the want of trying on Serena's part, I hear."

The revelation was devastating for Laura. Had she totally misjudged Blake? She now felt remorseful for leaving Barbados without saying goodbye to him. *I felt I had it all worked out, knew what I was doing,* she thought. *But it looks like I didn't have a clue.*

Emma put her glass of wine carefully down on the coffee table. Leaning back in her chair, she focused her gaze on Laura. She spoke candidly.

"You told me you and Blake were just friends."

"We were – until we weren't."

"I guess that happens," said Emma. "You're in love with Blake, aren't you?"

Laura was taken by surprise. Her cheeks flushed as the blood rushed through her veins. She realised that sometimes, friends know you better than you think. She remained quiet, not sure how to respond, until after a tearful sigh she unburdened herself to Emma.

"Which is why saying goodbye broke my heart."

"So you told Blake you were leaving?"

"No, I'm too much of a coward. That night I knew any possibility of a future with Blake was over. I had been kidding myself. I left without telling him." Laura's eyes filled with tears.

"You could have confided in me," said Emma. "Sometimes, friends can give you a new insight."

"Having you here has helped me. A good friend that I can talk to." It was the first time she had confided her feelings for Blake to Emma and the emotion crushed her.

"Come back to Barbados, Laura, we all miss you."

"I miss everyone too, but it's too early. There are some things I still need to work through."

"And how's that going?" Emma asked pointedly.

"Not well," admitted Laura.

"Why give up everything in Barbados and hide away here on Holy Island?"

"Because I knew it was all too good to be true," sighed Laura.

"You know, Laura, you can't win when you're fighting yourself."

They were both quiet. A despondency had fallen over the evening.

"It all seems so hopeless," Emma sighed.

"We need more wine," said Laura, trying to lift the mood.

"Bring the bottle," Emma called after her.

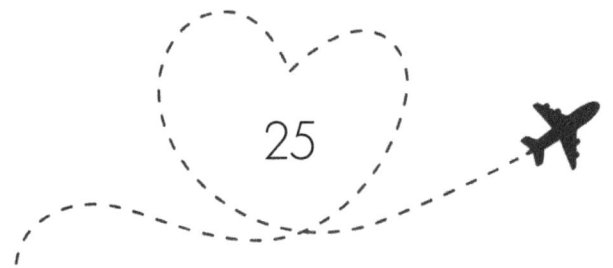

25

The small beach cafe near Carlisle Bay was playing soft reggae music as Blake and Charlie sat in the air con at a quiet corner table drinking lattes. Charlie sat with his back to the wall. The beach was busy. Through the window he could see a pontoon at the water's edge unloading passengers from a pleasure boat. Tourists wandered by the window in shorts and swimsuits, looking for an umbrella on the beach to relax under. Two things had become apparent to Charlie: firstly, Blake was in a downcast frame of mind, and secondly, there was no contract from Toronto.

"So no green light as yet?" Charlie asked, taking a sip of coffee.

"Looks that way," replied Blake. Taking his shades off, he looked tired. "Before talks were finalised, it all kicked off in New York!"

"Yes, I'm sorry to hear about your father."

"He's slowly recovering," said Blake.

"Good news," said Charlie. "What about this Canadian company?" he continued. "You say it's world class."

"It is," replied Blake. "There's an urgency to transport medical supplies whilst maintaining their existing routes, opening a niche in the market for freighters like us. They provide a leasing and maintenance service, fuel management and much more. We get access to more airports."

"You made it clear – no dangerous goods or hazardous materials?" Charlie asked.

"Of course. Their handlers ensure the consignments are ready for carriage in compliance with regs and import-export rules for countries in transit."

"Well," said Charlie, "the margins are certainly good. So why do I detect a lack of enthusiasm?"

"You may not like what I have to say," replied Blake.

"Try me," said Charlie.

"I've been doing a lot of soul-searching since my father had the heart attack. I don't want to end up like him. I think I've been competing with him, determined to prove I don't need him. I've lost myself in there somewhere." Blake took a deep breath and looked at Charlie.

"We only have one life, Charlie. My family have more than enough money for several lifetimes. Do we need all those zeros?"

"This is unexpected," said Charlie, sitting back in his seat to consider the implications of what he'd just heard.

"I think we should run the company to fit with our values, do things our way," said Blake.

"Don't we already do that?" asked Charlie.

"I mean in a way that gives us time to be with family, friends, time to do things we enjoy, time to embrace life."

"I thought you thrived on the cut and thrust," said Charlie.

Blake heaved a sigh. "Not anymore, Charlie. Not anymore. I don't want company business to rule my life. I don't want to be away from home for weeks at a time, flying or chasing deals."

"Talk about getting your house in order, Blake."

"It's been a rough few weeks," Blake said wearily.

"Suits me," said Charlie. "I'm about to become a dad. I never knew mine. I want to be there – be involved." Charlie said it with such quiet resolution Blake could feel the stress lift from his shoulders.

"This Canadian deal – do we really want to stretch ourselves so far?" asked Blake.

"I think we both know the answer to that," replied Charlie.

Charlie took a long look at Blake; he saw the relief in his eyes. He suspected, however, that it wasn't the only thing Blake wanted to discuss, but he didn't want to drag it out of him. There was a long gap in the conversation. Charlie was about to ask, "So what's up?" when Blake cleared his throat.

"There's something else," he said.

"I'm guessing this is about affairs of the heart," Charlie grinned.

"Well, I may have lost my head as well," said Blake.

"We've all been guilty of that," smiled Charlie.

The two men had a strong friendship, but they rarely discussed women. Blake knew he could rely on Charlie to be downright honest with him.

"I think I've grown up with a skewed vision of what love is," began Blake. "I saw it as controlling, even destructive. I haven't had much to go on. In fact, being with my family, I sometimes feel like I'm in my own personal combat zone." He gave a wry smile. "But this is about Laura."

"I thought as much," said Charlie.

Blake was surprised. "What makes you say that?"

"I may live in Trinidad, Blake, but I haven't been living under a rock."

Blake took a deep breath. "I can hardly keep pace with what's happening. Things have moved so quickly. Laura is your sister; you have found each other. I think that's amazing, I know how much it means to you. But since you told me I can't help wondering if this changes things between us." Blake looked anxiously at Charlie.

"Why should it? Laura is a special person, part of my family, I love her and will always watch out for her. She is an independent woman and I respect that. You and I are old friends, Blake."

Another long pause.

"So, what *about* Laura?" Charlie prompted.

"Before I met her, I had no fear of ending a relationship because a partner was easily replaceable. But Laura is different."

"Are you finally admitting a connection you've never felt with anyone before?"

"I've never told a girl I loved her. I never got that far before if that's what you mean? I've lived this way for a long time. Then I meet one person and everything changes, I feel out of control."

"That's how it happens," said Charlie. "So you've learnt how to love, it's been a long time coming. It's not me you should be telling. You should have already talked to Laura about this."

"I tried at the party, a big mistake. It didn't go well."

"At a party? Who are you trying to convince?" scoffed Charlie.

"I haven't found the right moment. The next morning I left for Toronto."

"You ran away, took to the skies when life got too intense," said Charlie.

Blake realised that it was just possible that his behaviour had been insensitive to say the least.

"I think I took life for granted – I didn't appreciate the important things. Now I've lost her. I don't know what to do."

"You were always moving on, Blake, you like a quick turnaround. Always seeking pleasure, not meaning. Suddenly it got too real. It's not all about you anymore, or the notches on your bed. You're in love and you panicked. A relationship takes commitment and responsibility."

Blake had expected Charlie to be blunt; he needed that. How well Charlie knew him.

"You're right, Charlie, I don't know what a real relationship looks like."

Charlie had never seen Blake like this before, heard him speak in this way. He seemed lost.

"You're not going to let Laura slip through your fingers, are you? Be left wondering *what if*?"

Blake remained silent.

"You can't duck this one, Blake," said Charlie quietly.

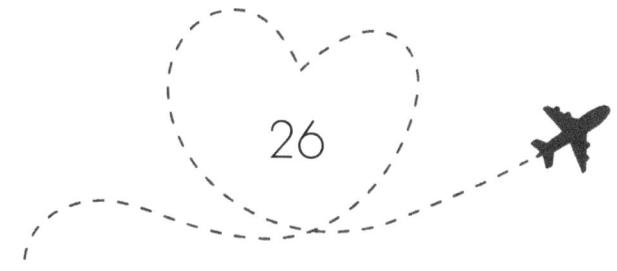

26

The conversation with Emma and the news of Blake had disturbed Laura. The realisation that she may have misread so much and judged Blake too harshly now weighed on her mind. She should have listened to her heart, she should have listened to Blake. Instead, she had allowed her insecurities to run away with her. Now she had lost so much that was dear to her. The regret was overwhelming but, like the truth, had it come too late?

After dark on Friday night Laura was thankful that most of the sorting was done. Exhausted with a weariness that came deep from within, she took a hot bath, filling it with lavender essence in the hope she would be blessed with sleep that night. Putting on her dressing gown, she went through to her bedroom. Looking out onto the still clear night, she saw that the frost sparkled on the ground. Laura thought how peaceful it all was. The windows of the cottages across the narrow street were masked by drawn curtains. In the distance she heard a dog bark, eerily disturbing the stillness. Pulling the cream linen curtains together, she was about to turn out the light when the dog barked again at the same time as the doorbell rang. Laura felt slightly unnerved. Cautiously, she pulled the front door inwards to open it. As she did so, a blast of cold night air hit her face. Peering out into the darkness her heart leapt, because there, huddled in the shadows, was Blake!

"Sorry to come unannounced," he said softly.

"What are you doing here?" Laura's heart was thumping in her chest.

"I'm here to see you, Laura. Can I come in?"

The low, calm tones of his voice soothed her. The voice she had missed so much, the voice she had longed to hear again but thought she never would. Blake looked tired and drawn. Laura could sense his fatigue as he stepped into the room.

"How are you, Laura?"

"I'm fine," she replied evenly. But she was not fine; she was as far away from fine as it is possible to be – she was overwrought. Trying to keep a facade of calm to hide the panic she felt inside, Laura began to remove a few of her things from the sofa to make room for Blake to sit down. She tried to sound matter-of-fact.

"The room isn't usually this untidy, I am just sorting out the cottage."

"It's okay, Laura." Blake took off his overcoat and, hanging it over the arm of the sofa, he sat down.

"Can I get you coffee or something to warm you through?" Laura asked.

"I'm good, thanks. I checked into the hotel at the causeway until crossing time."

"I was sorry to hear about your father," she said. It was the first thing that came into her head. She didn't tell him how she knew and he didn't ask.

"He's recovering. It was a warning shot. It's made him reassess his life. He's discovered he has a family who love him. Now he's learning to delegate at the ripe age of 61," Blake chuckled lightly.

Laura wanted to ask about Kristina but thought better of it. This wasn't exactly a social catch-up visit. Something in Blake's demeanour and body language told her that all was not well. Blake's eyes held hers for only a brief moment before he turned away. Those eyes that she loved so much now made her feel uneasy, because she saw in them the anguish he was feeling. Tentatively, she sat down beside him as he began to speak.

"Maybe in Barbados I was too focused on my own needs, Laura. I've tormented myself with how I made it look as though I was only interested in the physical." His voice was unsteady; he was trying to keep his emotions under control. He turned to look at her.

"There was so much I wanted to say to you but the time never seemed right. When I returned from New York to find you'd left Barbados, it was like a hammer blow to the chest. I went into free fall."

Laura had never heard Blake speak this way before. He was never overwhelmed, it was not in his DNA. She felt her heart pulsing in her throat. No way had she been prepared for such intensity. Blake put his hand on top of hers.

"I'm in love with you, Laura. I've never said that to anyone before."

Laura struggled to digest what she was hearing.

"I didn't know, Blake, you didn't tell me." Her voice was trembling as much as her heart.

"I don't find it easy to say what I'm feeling; I couldn't bring myself to admit it." Blake's voice was low and strained.

"But I needed to hear it," Laura said softly.

She saw a muscle tense in Blake's cheek and a flicker of uncertainty in his eyes.

Blake had flown four thousand miles and had placed his heart and his pride in Laura's hands. If she rejected him now, that would be the end of it, but he had to take that chance. Reaching into the breast pocket of his jacket, he took out a small box and opened the lid to reveal a white gold band set with a single solitaire diamond.

"It belonged to my grandmother. When she gave it to me, she made me promise I would only give it to the woman I love."

His words made Laura catch her breath; she had not expected this in a million years. Her gaze fell to the ring. It was elegant and beautiful. She saw Blake swallow; he got down on one knee, holding the ring towards her.

"From the moment I met you, I knew you were special. I can't imagine my life without you. What I'm trying to say is, Laura Stevens, will you marry me?"

She saw those brown eyes that set her heart aquiver. She understood the emotion that was surging through him because it surged through her too. She fought back the tears. She whispered softly, "Yes."

Blake took her hand and placed the ring on her finger. His arms folded around her.

"I love you so much, Laura." His voice was choked and his eyes prickled with tears; he couldn't hold them back.

In the pale light of the bedroom the moon shone softly through the curtains. Laura lay on the bed and watched Blake undress. His tanned body was beautiful, toned and muscular. He leaned over and lay on his side, facing her. Taking off her robe, his fingers twined her hair and came down the nape of her neck tenderly to her breasts. Feeling the electric tingle of his skin on hers, the warm sensation within her, Laura sighed with happiness. She put her arms around his neck. Blake moved closer to her.

"This has been on my mind for so long, I've missed you so damned much," he said.

"I've missed you too, Blake, more than you'll ever know. There's been an emptiness deep inside me that nothing seemed to fill."

Blake smiled. "Let me see if I can fix that," he murmured huskily.

And suddenly, the little cottage on Holy Island was as warm as the white sands of Barbados.

Epilogue

The wedding was everything Laura and Blake wanted it to be. Their emotional journey was culminating today in the little Church of St. Aidan on the beach at Bathsheba in the presence of those they loved.

Dulcie entered the church first in a long, iris-blue dress, scattering rose petals from a basket as she walked. Emma followed as maid of honour, also in blue. Heads turned as Laura walked down the aisle on the arm of a proud Marvin. Her dress of ivory silk was simple and stunning. She looked radiant. Blake was waiting for her at the altar, his eyes moist with emotion. Charlie stood beside him, keeping the rings. Blake glanced tenderly at Laura by his side; she smiled, he touched her arm lightly – a small gesture that conveyed so much.

The sun shone through the beautiful stained-glass window as Blake took her hand in his and they made their vows. You could hear a pin drop as Liam solemnised their marriage. Afterwards, as they were leaving the church, the sounds of congratulatory voices and laughter rose as everyone gathered outside for photographs. William and Rhonda hugged and kissed them both, genuinely happy for them. Monica was smiling broadly; due to give birth in a few weeks, she was thrilled to have made it to the wedding of her baby's godparents. Before long, a row of white limos arrived to transport them all to Cliffside, which had been set up solely for their use on this special day. The chef had carefully prepared a menu to suit their tastes. Eugene and his staff lined up outside to welcome everyone with a glass of champagne.

The wedding tables were covered with white cloths and bowls of blue and white flowers. There was delicious food and, of course, speeches. Marvin was in his element. There was more food and cake. Laura and Blake took to the floor to the applause of the guests for the first dance. "Let's Stay Together", chosen by Blake. Then, as the music changed, there was an outburst of dancing as the party began. Laura looked around at all the happy faces: Ivan and Carmel, Erika, Marc and Aylen with Fidel, who was looking dapper in his new suit. Rudy and Myrtle, everyone was there. She caught sight of Kristina dancing with Sean. He seemed so settled these days, so happy with life. Kristina was laughing; *who wouldn't in Sean's company?* she mused.

Laura went out onto the terrace to have a moment alone. The air was surprisingly cool. The overtures from inside floated into the background. Resting her hands on the rail, she looked up at the sky. The sun had set and the moon provided that half-light that makes everything seem so perfect. The tree frogs were beginning their nightly chorus. Below, she could hear the waters of the Atlantic Ocean as they crashed to shore. She loved evenings like this. She was mindful of the first day she had arrived in Barbados, how much had begun on that day that would change her life forever. She thought of David and the painting of Lindisfarne Castle he'd sent her as a wedding present. The picture she loved now hung in the hallway of the beach house. A reminder of the island in the North Sea where she had grown up.

Laura stood for a while, thinking about her marriage. All the formalities, the solemn vows she and Blake had made to one another. Tonight, she had the feeling of coming home, a feeling of no longer being alone, a feeling of happiness. Blake came out to the terrace to join her. He put his hand over hers.

"You okay, Laura?"

"I'm okay," she smiled. Leaning back, she snuggled into his chest.

"Remember our first meeting at the airport?" he asked.

"As if it were yesterday," she whispered.

"Thank you for flying into my life," Blake said softly.

"My pleasure," she replied.

"Now we begin a new journey together. I love you, Laura Degas," he said, drawing her close to him.

Under the beautiful evening sky over Barbados, Blake took her in his arms and pressed his lips to hers in a long and intimate kiss.